Dear Reader,

As we enter our fifth decade of publishing quality romance fiction, we're proud to bring you our 3000th Harlequin Romance.

The Harlequin family includes a great many talented authors and artists. But our most important family member is you—the reader. We've always been able to count on you to tell us what you like in Harlequin Romances now...and what you want to see in them in the future.

Thanks to you, Harlequin Romance has a reputation for publishing contemporary stories that celebrate love while reflecting strong traditional values. Stories that can move you to laughter and tears...and leave you feeling good inside.

THE LOST MOON FLOWER, our 3000th Harlequin Romance, is a richly romantic adventure we hope you'll enjoy today.

Just as we hope you'll spare a few moments from your busy life to share with us your comments and opinions for the Harlequin Romances of tomorrow.

Sincerely,

The Editors

Harlequin Romance
225 Duncan Mill Road
Don Mills, Ontario
M3B 3K9

She stood beside him in awkward silence

Whitewater leaned toward her, putting his mouth so close to her ear that the warmth seemed to burn her skin. "Do you want to tell me what kind of trouble you're in?"

Fatigue and befuddlement fell away from her, replaced by wariness. "I never said I was in trouble," Josie replied, her voice slightly choked.

He folded his arms across his chest and glanced down at her coolly. "You're in trouble, all right. Big trouble. *Wasichu*—as my Sioux granddad used to say. More than can be counted, I'd guess."

She tried to keep her chin from trembling. "How can you be so sure?"

He leaned close again. "I used a great power I have," he said mysteriously. "The name I give this power," he said, tapping his forehead, "is logic. Something has to be seriously amiss. What else could reduce you to saying you want me?"

The Lost Moon Flower

Bethany Campbell

Harlequin Books

TORONTO • NEW YORK • LONDON
AMSTERDAM • PARIS • SYDNEY • HAMBURG
STOCKHOLM • ATHENS • TOKYO • MILAN

ISBN 0-373-03000-2

Harlequin Romance first edition August 1989

CHAPTER ONE

FOR FIVE LONG GRAY days the Chicago wind had been wailing. February snow swept the city with frequent squalls.

In the whole of Chicago perhaps the only beings who were grateful for the weather were at the zoo. Among them were the polar bears, the Tibetan yaks, the arctic wolves—and an extremely unhappy young woman named Josie Talbott.

Everything was over for Josie, and she knew it. She was ruined, and her own sister had done it. She was glad for the snow, for hardly any visitors braved the blizzardy weather to visit the zoo. She was leaving her office for good today, closing its door for the last time. She didn't want anyone to see the effort it took to hold back her tears. She wasn't sure she ever wanted to see a human being again.

The office door swung shut and automatically locked. Its soft click had a terrible finality about it. Josie stared for the last time at its frosted glass window. Josie A. Talbott, Assistant Keeper, Panda House, said the black letters. Soon her name would be removed forever. She had already turned in her key. She was through. Her career was finished.

She shifted the box in her arms awkwardly. It held the last articles she had cleaned from her desk, including the little porcelain panda that had sat on her desk. Its presence seared through the box in which it was packed, through Josie's mittens and the thick sleeves of her jacket.

When she opened the back door of the panda house, an icy blast of wind slapped her face. She set her jaw, almost welcoming the pain. It gave her an excuse to let the tears sting her blue eyes.

The zoo officials, she knew, were also grateful for this powerful fit of Chicago's fabled weather. It kept people away from the zoo and away from the panda house.

The scolding gales whipped at her muffler, tossed her auburn curls. She hardly noticed. Her heart was so harrowed, her mind so numbed with betrayal, that the earth itself might blow away, dissolve into nothingness, and she wouldn't notice.

Her job was lost. Her future was ruined. That wasn't the worst of it. The worst was that she had disgraced the zoo, her profession, her city—even her country.

The republic of China, in a gesture of friendship, had given the zoo two of the rarest mammals in the world: a pair of giant pandas, Nan Wu and Yueh Hua— Wizard and Moon Flower.

Because of her, Josie Talbott, the priceless female panda had been stolen. The final shame was that Josie's own sister, Bettina, had helped abduct Moon Flower.

Josie struggled with the half-frozen lock of her little blue Chevrolet. She coaxed the stalwart engine of the small car to life. Only half-seeing, she drove between the weaving veils of snow.

Why had she been foolish enough to believe that her younger sister had changed at last? Why had she been gullible enough to get Bettina a job at the zoo?

Yet how could she have foreseen the enormity of Bettina's folly? For Moon Flower was not only one of the rarest animals in the world; she was pregnant, zoo officials were nearly certain. She might deliver in more than a month—or in a week. Much was still unknown in the breeding of pandas, but the hoped-for birth was to be a victory in the battle to keep the giant panda from extinction.

Josie negotiated the slippery streets automatically, heading toward her small overpriced apartment. The apartment was lovely, but more costly than she could afford. She had leased it primarily because it was close to the zoo.

Now it no longer mattered where she lived. She would not be called back to the panda house again. For two years, she had lived, breathed, thought and dreamed pandas. Wizard and Moon Flower had been her obsession, and a more enchanting obsession never existed, she was sure.

She pulled into the snowy parking lot of her building. Numbly she unloaded the car as the wind flayed her. Both she and Dr. Hazard, who supervised the panda house, considered the two pandas as a sacred trust. And both dreamed the same dream: to solve the problem that threatened the giant pandas' existence, which was the difficulty of breeding the animals in captivity.

When after two years of trying, the most accurate tests indicated that Moon Flower was probably carrying a baby panda, Josie and Dr. Hazard had locked themselves in his office and split a bottle of champagne. It had been the happiest day of her life. Now Moon Flower was gone. Her own sister had helped hijack her.

Josie didn't bother to hang up her coat or muffler or put away her cap and mittens. She moved in a daze, setting the cardboard box far back in her coat closet, not wanting to look at it. She particularly didn't want to look at the little porcelain panda. She couldn't stand it.

Not bothering to turn on the lights, she opened the curtains and stared out. Night was swiftly clamping down over Chicago, bringing iron darkness.

For the thousandth time she cursed herself for believing in Bettina. How had it come to this? she asked herself, shaking her head. She drew the curtains again and switched on a lamp. The room was neglected, reflecting the disorder in her mind. She stared into the mirror over the dark green velvet couch.

A tall slim woman with curling auburn hair and haunted blue-green eyes stared back at her. A smattering of freckles, left over from summer, seemed carefree and out of place on the bridge of her slim nose. She studied herself with dislike. It seemed almost as if her sister were looking at her from the mirror.

The two of them were so alike, yet so different. It had never bothered Josie that they had traveled so much when they were young. Their father, a wildlife photographer, had shown them much of the world, and Josie had found it rich with marvels.

Bettina, on the other hand, had found the world a place of threats and tension. Both girls had been shaken when their mother died of a fever in Africa. But Bettina, younger and more dependent, had never really recovered.

Bettina grew up looking much like Josie, only smaller, thinner and with hair a lighter, more intense red. Their eyes seemed the same turquoise color until one looked closely. Josie's eyes were always full of curiosity, confidence and laughter. Bettina's were full of needs, secrets and fears.

Their father had died suddenly when Josie was twenty-three and starting graduate school at Stanford. Bettina was eighteen, just beginning college in Boston. Josie had mourned him deeply, then gathered her forces and set out to live the kind of life that would make her father proud. But Bettina had never been the same.

Only slowly did it become apparent how troubled Bettina was. She flunked out of first one school, then another. She took up with this cause, then dropped it for that. She became involved with one wild-eyed young man after another.

By the time Josie came to Chicago, Bettina had dropped out of school completely and picked up with her strangest young man yet: Lucas Panpaxis. Josie had met him once and had immediately been frightened for her sister. Something in his eyes made Josie think he could be truly dangerous.

Lucas's real name was Wilber Lumpkin, but he had rechristened himself Lucas Panpaxis, saying the Greek name meant "light of world accord." He always wore black, including a black bandanna tied about his head—a symbol of mourning, he claimed, for all the injustice in the world.

He was a thin, twitchy, long-haired boy, who talked incoherently about everything that was wrong with society. He didn't bother working, saying he had greater things to accomplish. Josie had found him particularly sinister because one of his passions was flying; his mother kept buying him planes. Josie flinched to think of someone as weird as Lucas winging his way through the skies.

When Bettina and Lucas broke up, Josie had been profoundly relieved. She was flattered when Bettina asked if she could come join her. She sent her sister money to come to Chicago, and got her a job as assistant to one of the zookeepers. It wasn't a glamorous job, but it was low-pressure, and that, Bettina insisted, was what she needed.

Josie had loaned Bettina money, helped her find an apartment, talked with her about the past and the future. She'd thought everything was going fine—which showed precisely how little Josie knew.

For it was Lucas and Bettina and, authorities thought, at least two others, who had kidnapped Moon Flower last Sunday night. How they got through the zoo's security system no one knew. No one was even sure why they had kidnapped the animal.

What crazed scheme was galloping through Lucas's head could hardly be imagined. Nobody knew whether Bettina had been in league with Lucas from the time she came to Chicago, or if he had somehow found her and exerted his old charm on her. Only one thing was certain: Moon Flower was gone. Lucas and Bettina had taken her. And they had used Josie's key to get into the panda house.

The five days since the betrayal and theft had been hell for Josie. Neither the zoo nor the authorities wanted any word of the crime to leak out. First, they didn't want to intoxicate Lucas with the wine of publicity. Second, they didn't want to give anyone else ideas; the prospect of a wave of rare animals stolen and held for ransom was too forbidding. And third, the incident was humiliating, not only on a national, but an international, level.

For five numbing, endless days Josie had been questioned by everyone; the police, the FBI, even a representative from the State Department. She didn't know how the FBI was so certain it was Lucas who had masterminded the crime, but she was sure they were right.

The group had drugged the panda, the FBI believed, and taken her aboard a small plane, whose destination was supposed to be Mexico. But Lucas's plane had never arrived in Mexico. Nobody knew where it had gone. Or where Moon Flower was.

Bettina, how could you? Josie asked silently. *Lucas, what do you think you're doing?* But the questions that tortured her most were: *Moon Flower, are you all right? Are you still alive? Do you still have your baby?*

Josie loved the panda as she had never loved any animal, even more than Wizard, Moon Flower's clownish and crowd-pleasing mate. Moon Flower's loss created a terrible emptiness in her, a kind of death.

The apartment was cold, she noticed vaguely, but she didn't bother to turn up the heat. She sat on the green velvet couch and hugged herself helplessly.

Everything was broken and ruined. Her own sister was a fugitive, Moon Flower was stolen and in danger, or perhaps already dead. Josie couldn't stand to think of the baby panda. For the first time in her life, she was glad her father was not alive; he had been spared seeing this.

An urgent knock rattled the door of the apartment. She shuddered slightly, trying to bring herself back to reality. She opened the door with trepidation. For the past five days she had talked only to the authorities and zoo officials.

Her neighbor, Mrs. Mollie Spotts, a tiny woman of indeterminate age, stood there. Her pointed little face looked up at Josie in ill-disguised worry.

"Josie," she said, her black eyes frankly troubled, "I have a long-distance phone call for you. I'm sure it's Bettina. She insists you talk to her on *my* phone. Is something wrong?"

Josie froze. "Bettina?" she repeated numbly. Mollie nodded curtly, watching Josie's stunned expression.

Bettina, thought Josie. She was calling through Mollie Spotts because she knew that Josie's own phone might be tapped by authorities. "Good heavens," she breathed raggedly. Then she was out the door, unaware that she was running down the hall in her stocking feet, or that she simply pushed her way into Mollie's apartment, leaving Mollie behind.

She seized the phone. "Bettina?" she said desperately, her heart beating hard. "Is this you? Where are you? Where's Moon Flower? How is she? What, in the name of all that's holy, do you and Lucas think—"

"Josie, please don't be angry," begged Bettina. She sounded close to tears. "We didn't mean any harm. Honest!"

Don't be angry. We didn't mean any harm, Josie thought in furious disbelief. "Bettina, where's Moon Flower?" she demanded. "Is she all right?"

"She's all right. She's fine . . . so far," Bettina said in the same choked voice. The connection was bad, as if Bettina were half a world away. "Listen, Josie, I can't talk long. We took the panda because Lucas said it'd make people listen to his ideas. We were going to hold her hostage until certain demands were met—"

"Demands? What demands?" questioned Josie, thinking this was it, this was the call everybody had been waiting for. Her sister was going to tell her what Lucas wanted in exchange for Moon Flower.

"Well," Bettina said lamely, "we thought...just certain demands—like outlawing live traps for animals, and banning pesticides and herbicides...to stop poisoning the environment...all over the world, but..."

Oh heaven, thought Josie, rubbing her forehead. Leave it to Lucas to think he could wipe out all the pain and pollution in the world by stealing one helpless pregnant panda.

"But," Bettina went on, the same hurt catch in her voice, "now that Lucas has her, well, he thinks he might demand more. He thinks he can make anybody do whatever he wants, because if they don't..."

Bettina's weak voice gave way. The pause was ominous. Josie heard the call of a bird.

"If they don't do what he wants, he'll what?" Josie prodded.

"He'll...hurt her." Bettina sniffled.

She means he'll kill her, Josie thought with horrified certainty.

"Josie, I didn't know it'd go this far. He's thinking over his demands now. He wants to announce them a week from today, because it'll be Friday the thirteenth—people will remember that day. It'll make them think—"

"Don't let him touch her," Josie ordered, terrified. She could hardly imagine anyone evil enough to hurt her beautiful Moon Flower, but Lucas had gone this far. Who knew where he might stop? "Bettina, you can't let him harm her, do you hear me? No matter what happens, you can't let him hurt her, do you understand?"

"Yes," Bettina answered, weeping openly now, "but I'm scared, Josie. I'm scared of what we've done and I'm scared of Lucas and—"

"Where are you?" Josie demanded. "I'll help you. I'll get help—"

"We came to a village . . . for supplies," Bettina replied, and snuffled again. "I don't know exactly where this place is—we're hidden away up where nobody can find us—but I think it's—"

Josie heard Bettina give a little cry, as if in fear or pain. There was another sinister silence on the phone, broken only by the call of the same bird. The bird sounded idiotically cheerful.

Then she heard Lucas's voice growling through the wire. "Josie?" he said, his tone strained and excited. "She shouldn't have done that. I mean, the minute my back is turned, she loses her nerve. The *minute* my back is turned."

"Lucas . . ." Josie pleaded, but her mind was spinning with one dreadful certainty: he was crazy. He was crazy and he had her sister and Moon Flower. "I'll do whatever you want, Lucas," she said desperately.

"You bet you will," he answered. His voice had a self-dramatizing whine. "And what you'll do is keep quiet. This call never happened, hear me? If I see anybody coming near this place, I'll know you talked, and that means kiss it all goodbye, big sister, kiss it all goodbye. The panda's gone for good."

"I won't tell anybody," Josie insisted in panic. "Just don't hurt anybody, Lucas—or anything. Take time. Think carefully."

"I'm taking time," Lucas retorted in the same tense whine. "I'll announce what I want in one week—on Friday the thirteenth. But I mean it, Josie, you keep quiet about this call, and if anybody has a tap on this phone, tell them to stay away—or else. I mean it."

"There's no tap on the phone," Josie said placatingly. "Bettina's not stupid. This isn't my phone."

"Just remember," Lucas warned. "You don't tell anybody. Nobody comes near us. The panda's history. Even your own sister might not be so safe. It's in your hands now, Josie. It's your responsibility. If anything goes wrong, it's your fault."

My fault for ever trying to help Bettina, she thought with helpless anger, but she dared not say it. She waited for Lucas to give her more orders, to make more self-aggrandizing statements, but the line went dead.

She stared numbly at the phone. She punched the receiver button. "Hello? Hello?" The line hummed emptily.

Mollie Spotts stood by the doorway, looking at her with a furrowed brow. "Josie," she said, closing the door behind her, "you're in trouble, aren't you? Where's Bettina? I haven't seen her for a couple of days, and you've been like a hermit. What's wrong? Can you tell me? I'm here if you need a friend."

Dully, Josie put the receiver back in place. She looked down into Mollie's kindly pointed face. "I'm sorry," she said, biting her lower lip. "I can't tell you, Mollie. I just...can't, that's all. Thanks for coming to get me."

Tears blurred her eyes. She tried to shrug to indicate she was all right, but somehow the gesture didn't work. She shook her head wordlessly. She walked past Mollie and opened the door.

"I'm sorry," she repeated, and hated herself for leaving Mollie staring after her with such helpless concern.

Slowly she walked down the hall. She entered her apartment and sat down on the couch and stared at the phone. She could call the authorities, she thought fatalistically, but she was frightened. She knew Lucas well enough to know he meant what he said: if he found out she'd told anyone, the worst would happen. She could count on it.

Besides, she thought, her head aching, she knew nothing really, except that Moon Flower was still all right. For now.

If only, she thought hopelessly, there was some way to get to Moon Flower and Bettina and slip away with them before Lucas knew or could do any harm. But that was impossible. She didn't even know where they were.

A village, Bettina had said. That was all. A village where there was a phone. It could be anywhere.

Josie sat up half the night, shivering slightly in the cold room and simply staring into the darkness. Her thoughts seemed to lose all coherence. Sometimes she thought of nothing at all, as if her brain had died. At other times, irrelevant memories took over, and numbly she let them. It was like being held captive in a movie house where someone else had charge of the projector.

Most of the memories were of her father or Moon Flower. Some were of Bettina. And one that kept haunting her had no relevance at all. It was about the time she'd made a fool of herself on television.

The pointless recollection ran in her head like an embarrassing and disjointed film. Helplessly she let it. Maybe, she thought, she was going crazy.

Last year, one of the television stations had initiated a talk show called *Chicago Takes Sides*. Josie, like Bettina, had strong beliefs. Unlike Bettina, she hoped, she never took hers to harmful extremes. But one thing she believed in strongly was that hunting animals was wrong. Her career was given to preserving threatened species. She could not condone hunting; she hated it.

The station asked her to take a stand against a professional sportsman, a man named Aaron Whitewater. Josie had agreed with relish. After all, she had been the captain of her college debating team— undefeated for three straight years. She would make Aaron Whitewater look like the insensitive, violence- loving lunk that he was.

The host, Rex Bartholomew, said that Whitewater was not only a big game hunter, but a fisherman and tracker. A quiet man, he warned, but blunt and with an acid sense of humor; he was not to be underestimated.

Bartholomew was right. Josie knew she was in trou- ble the moment she met Whitewater. She had expected a boasting macho type dressed in full safari gear, an el- ephant gun by his side. He would have blood thirst in his heart, slaughter in his eye and an IQ slightly lower than a brick.

She'd walked into the studio's greenroom before the show, looking every inch The Friendly Representative from the Zoo. Her dark red hair was subdued for once. She wore a turquoise-blue wool suit that set off her clear eyes and made her cheeks seem wholesomely pink. She'd looked cheerful, capable and clean-cut to the point of being almost sexless.

Rex Bartholomew introduced her to Aaron Whitewater. Whitewater didn't look cheerful, he did look formidably capable, and he looked anything but sexless.

My, she thought with a zoologist's cool detachment, *that is an exceedingly fine male of the species.* She had never really paid too much attention to men: she had always been too involved in her career. Whitewater, however, was a hard man not to notice. But she immediately regained possession of herself. She smiled, once more The Friendly Representative from the Zoo.

He rose from his chair to shake her hand. He wore a tailor-made suit of charcoal gray, a conservative tie. Josie felt a tingle of excited danger. She was five feet nine inches tall, almost six feet in her high heels. But Aaron Whitewater towered a full six inches above her, all wide shoulders and tailored elegance.

She felt her hand swallowed up by his much larger one. His hair was so dark a brown it seemed black, as did his eyes. "I'm very pleased to meet you, Mr. Whitewater," she had said with mechanical politeness.

But he had already let go of her hand. "I doubt it," he said laconically. He sat down again, as if extremely bored, picked up a tattered copy of a magazine and perused it, as if last year's news were infinitely more interesting than Josie.

She blinked in surprise. Rex Bartholomew smiled weakly and left them together, going to check his set. Josie sat down stiffly on the edge of a couch opposite Aaron Whitewater's chair. She picked up a magazine even more ancient than his and pretended to study it.

Secretly she peeked past its dog-eared pages and stole another glance at him. He was one of those big men, so well constructed that he did not give the impression of massiveness, but simply of power and grace. His thick dark hair had a slight wave to it, and she imagined that if it were left to its own devices, it would fall over his forehead, shadowing his rather exotic-looking black eyes.

He had an aquiline nose, a strong jaw and a chin that jutted slightly. His skin was bronzed, even though it was winter, his dark brows were straight, and his well-shaped mouth was set in an inflexible line. But it was his cheekbones that arrested Josie. They were high and strong and somehow alien to the expensive suit, the carefully barbered hair, the gold watch that winked from his brown wrist.

Good grief, thought Josie, he was a Native American—at least part. The last time she'd seen a set of cheekbones like that they had belonged to an Apache chief.

She felt at an immediate disadvantage. It was one thing to debate hunting with a man. It seemed, however, it might be another to debate hunting with a man whose racial heritage was hunting, and whose hunting grounds had been seized by her own race. Nonsense, she told herself, it made no difference.

But it did. Once they were on camera, he used the fact that he was half-Sioux with astounding subtlety and guile. He used, in fact, every trick in the debating book and a few he'd developed on his own.

He had been a devastating opponent, giving two facts for every one of hers, making her arguments sound silly and sentimental. Hunters, according to Aaron Whitewater, were the most dedicated conservationists in America. Who, after all, could be more interested in preserving species than those who wanted them plentiful enough to hunt?

Josie argued hotly. Too hotly. Aaron Whitewater's clipped delivery and the mocking gleam in his eye made her nervous, flustered, angry. She had never before felt so inadequate in an argument. Worse, she, who had always loathed violence, suddenly wanted nothing more than to hit him over the head.

When the show was over, she didn't want to stop the battle; she yearned to win at least one point from him. But he was through with her. He simply smiled. "You argue pretty well—for a woman," he said. Then he walked away.

Later, some said Aaron Whitewater had trounced Josie within an inch of her idealistic life, but others said she had stood her ground admirably. But she knew the truth: he had beaten her soundly. She smarted from it. She burned whenever she thought of him. The last time the Sioux had a victory like that, she secretly thought, had been at Little Bighorn. Whenever she thought of him, she squirmed.

Although she had never heard of Aaron Whitewater before, she seemed to notice his name all the time now. She heard he was hunting grizzlies in northern Alaska, fishing for shark off the coast of Georgia. She once heard that he'd flown to Saskatchewan, to join the search for a young deaf boy lost in the forest, and that he had actually tracked the child and saved him. Playing hero, she thought grudgingly....

She was surprised when she heard from Whitewater himself. Nearly six months after the show, she'd received a letter from Africa. From him. "Hello, Red," it said, scrawled in a bold stylized hand. "Came down here to check out a hyena problem. Started thinking of you. If you ever want to tangle again, let me know. Just say, 'Whitewater, I want you.'" In a postscript, he added his itinerary for the next six months, and a few addresses and phone numbers.

The gall! Josie had thought. She burned at being put next to the hyenas in his thoughts. His arrogance scalded. She crumpled the letter into a hard little ball and meant to throw it forcefully across her office.

But she hadn't thrown the note away. She had kept it, for some reason, in her desk drawer. She even remembered the itinerary: Kenya, Florida, then all winter in Hawaii; more fishing, hunting wild boar.

Hawaii, Josie thought without emotion. The blasted man was in Hawaii now. So what? She regretted he wasn't even farther away. The moon, for instance.

She didn't know why she was thinking of the obnoxious Whitewater or Hawaii, either. She was, she decided, really going crazy.

It was four o'clock in the morning, and her world seemed as cold and lifeless as the Chicago February howling outside her windows. Abruptly her thoughts veered back to Bettina's call. She remembered the desperation in Bettina's voice. She remembered the static on the wire, which made her sister sound so far away.

And she remembered the cry of the bird.

She had heard it quite clearly in the background when Bettina called. She had heard it twice. It had a strange, almost comical sound: *Tweety-po-wit. Tweety-po-wit.*

Josie felt so stunned that she saw stars swimming through the air. Hawaii, she thought. Of course. That's what her subconscious had been trying to tell her in its roundabout way by recalling Whitewater. *Hawaii.*

She was a zoologist. She knew what kind of bird made that cry: a kiki bird. And the kiki bird was native to but one place: the Kali Yin Islands, a small chain northeast of Hawaii. Bettina had said once that Lucas had spent part of his youth in Honolulu.

Bettina and Moon Flower and Lucas were hidden away somewhere in the Kali Yin Islands. By Hawaii.

She didn't bother to think about what time it was, either in Chicago or in the islands of the Pacific. A headlong and desperate plan blinded her to any such minor considerations. She knew where Moon Flower was, and she knew how to find her. Her unconscious had been trying to tell her. God bless the infinite complexities of the human mind, she thought.

She got the cardboard box from the hall closet, rummaged through it feverishly until she found what she wanted.

It took an eternity for her telephone call to go through. When it finally did, the phone at the other end seemed to ring forever. *Please,* she prayed. Please, please. Please answer.

At last the phone was picked up. She heard music in the background, Hawaiian music. "Hello," said a deep lazy voice.

For a moment Josie's heart thundered so hard she couldn't speak. But finally she managed to make her voice work. She uttered the words she had sworn she never would say. "Whitewater," she said shakily. "Whitewater, I want you."

CHAPTER TWO

"I WANT YOU, TOO, darling," said Whitewater. "Who is this, by the way?"

"Aaron Whitewater?" she asked, her voice still trembling. "This is Josie Talbott. I...I need you. I need you badly."

"Josie Talbott," he mused, as if he could not place the name. "Josie Talbott. The girl from New Zealand? Listen, love, I thought I told you—"

"Josie Talbott of Chicago," Josie practically wailed. "We had a fight. On television. Last February."

He paused, obviously trying to remember. "Right," he said at last. "And I won. What can I do for you? You're the blonde, right?"

"You did not win," she retorted. He had, but she still couldn't admit it aloud. "It was a draw, a tie. I'm a redhead. I need your help. This has got to be confidential. It's a matter of life and death."

"It usually is," he answered.

She thought she heard him suppress a yawn. She ignored it and forged on. "How well do you know the Kali Yin Islands?" she asked.

"Better than most," he drawled. "Not much game there. Not much of anything there except forests and mountains and waterfalls. What is it? You want me to take you camping or something?"

She recoiled at the chuckle in his voice. "No!" she retorted. "Well, yes...maybe. I don't know. Listen, Whitewater, could a small plane get from California to one of the Kali Yins?"

He seemed to turn the question over in his mind. "It's possible. A twin-engine rigged with extra fuel could do it. Or an old World War II number. People collect them. One of them could make it easily."

"How about landing?" Josie asked, pressing onward. "Do any of the Kail Yins have landing strips? Could they accommodate a plane big enough to make it from the mainland?"

"The biggest ones have strips," he answered impatiently. "More or less. They could accommodate a big twin-engine. An old plane like the DC-3 could land in a pasture, for that matter. What's this about? Are you calling to play Twenty Questions? Is there a point to this? It's the shank of the evening, you know. I have plans."

"I have to know all this," Josie answered, trying to keep the panic out of her voice. "Please. Help me."

"I love it when you say please," he said with amiable insolence. "I bet it's a word you hate to use with me. Say it again."

"Please." She winced in frustration. "If you went to one of the Kali Yins from the mainland, and you wanted to hide—you know, to stay undetected—where would you go?"

"More questions," he said with disgust. "Listen, I have a mai tai and a brunette waiting for me down in the bar."

"Please, Whitewater!"

"All right, all right. If I really knew what I was doing, and I assure you I do, I'd pick Kali Yushan—

Mount Jade. It's the most inaccessible. Very rough, very mountainous."

"And if you...didn't really know what you were doing?" urged Josie. "If you thought you were very smart, but were also kind of, uh, unbalanced, which one would you choose?"

"Lady," he muttered, "you ask the damnedest things. It's a beautiful night. The trees are full of orchids. The sky is full of moon. The surf is rolling in on the beach. And you want me to sit here and answer a crazy question like that?"

"Yes," she said humbly. "Please, Whitewater."

"Okay," he said with a sigh. "If I thought I was smart, but wasn't quite as smart as I thought I was, there's no question about it, I'd go to Kali Chenshan— the Stone Gate. It's bigger, not quite so untamed, and it's got one good-sized town."

The village, Josie thought with certainty. "With phone service to the mainland?" she asked.

"Yes. What do you want to know next? If they've got pizza delivery? A symphony orchestra? A wine-tasting club?"

"Whitewater, what would you charge to take me to Kali Chenshan?" Josie asked. Once more she could hear the tremor in her voice. Even with half a continent and half an ocean between them, Aaron Whitewater frightened her somehow. But she thought of Moon Flower, beautiful Moon Flower with her black mask and pretty face, and she forced herself to go on. "I want you to take me there. As soon as possible."

Only silence greeted her statement. She heard the music clearly in the background. A steel guitar twanged. A ukulele plunked.

"Whitewater?" she asked timidly. Had he simply dropped the phone and headed for his mai tai and his brunette?

"Why do you want me to take you to Chenshan?" he asked, skepticism in his husky voice. "Don't tell me you want to take up hunting?"

"No...not exactly. But kind of. A bit. Sort of. But not exactly. There's something I have to...find. I can't talk about it on the phone. I want to go immediately. If I get to Honolulu tomorrow, can you take me?"

Another long silence greeted her. "I'm all booked up. I'm supposed to be helping a guy who's writing an article on winter fishing in the islands. I've got a date with a swordfish. What can you offer that's better?"

She couldn't ignore the challenge in his voice. "Better than a fish?" she asked in disbelief. "Listen, I told you this is a matter of life and death—it's tremendously important. More important than I can tell you—"

"You don't understand. I have a commitment. I also *like* to fish."

Josie ran a hand through her auburn curls in frustration. "I'll pay you anything you want. Do you understand that? Anything. I'll sign my whole bank account over to you—my car, my television set, my mother's pearls, anything—if you'll just take me to Kali Chenshan and help me find what I have to find."

She heard him humming thoughtfully along with the music. "Let me see if I understand this," he said, and she could almost see the jeer on his bronzed face. "You just said, several times in fact, that you would give me *anything* I wanted if I helped you. Have I got it right?"

"You've got it," she agreed, teeth clenched. She didn't like his tone. It was too provocative. But her sister and Moon Flower and very possibly Moon Flower's baby were at stake. "Name it," she said. "It's yours."

"How about South Dakota?" he asked sarcastically. "As I recall, your people took it from my people, and my people were rather attached to it. Also North Dakota, Nebraska and Wyoming."

"Anything within reason, Whitewater," Josie muttered, suddenly remembering why she had hated him so much, "I'll give you anything I have. This is not a joking matter."

"Neither was South Dakota," he returned. "Remember Custer's Last Stand? Besides, I can't think of anything you've got that I want."

If Josie hadn't been so frightened and desperate, she would have told him precisely where she thought he would spend eternity and in what sorry state of salvation he would spend it. Instead she swallowed hard. She could feel her pride being forced down her throat, like a large bitter pill. "Please, Whitewater," she said for what seemed the hundredth time.

There was more silence. "Well," he said at last, and yawned distinctly, "Maybe. But say the rest of it. You know. What you said to me first."

She swallowed hard again. She thought of Bettina. She thought of Moon Flower's lovely, innocent face. "Please, Whitewater," she repeated, the words like ashes in her mouth, "I want you."

"I love it," he said.

But he promised he'd see her the next day. She hung up, exhausted yet strangely exhilarated. She glanced at her watch. It was four-thirty in the morning. She called O'Hare Airport.

"I'm coming, Moon Flower," she said aloud. "Bettina, you'll pay for this—somehow. In the meantime, take care of my panda. Whatever else you do, take care of my panda.''

MAGICALLY, THE SNOW seemed to clear just long enough for Josie's jet to take off from Chicago and climb above the gray clouds. She slept as much as she could on the flight, worn down by her long frightening week and worry-filled night.

When the jet began its final descent she awoke with a disbelieving heart. Outside the sky was blue, beneath it the sea was almost as blue, and the land was blanketed with thick rich green. The sun was shining so brightly it actually hurt her eyes.

She snapped open her compact. Her dark red curls seemed more unruly than usual. She tugged in vain to make them stay in place more decorously. Her face looked as pallid as a ghost's. That was appropriate, she thought ironically. The Josie Talbott of a week ago existed no more. Her life was gone. Instead there was this white-faced young woman with wary blue-green eyes and a plan she didn't want to think about too hard. She knew what she was doing was reckless, probably even foolhardy. But she could think of no other choice.

Groggily she applied a haphazard coat of pink lipstick, then powdered the freckles on her nose. She straightened her blouse and her travel-wrinkled suit jacket. She was, she noticed for the first time, wearing the same turquoise suit she'd had on the day she met and fought with Whitewater. When was that? A hundred years ago?

Whitewater. He was something else she didn't care to think about too deeply. She didn't know what she was getting into, becoming involved with him. But she knew if anyone could help her find and save Moon Flower, he was the one. Why she had such unshakable faith in him was not a question that even occurred to her.

She got off the plane and looked around the airport. People were embracing, families were reuniting, lovers were kissing. Except for the newly arrived tourists, everyone seemed sun-browned, relaxed and smiling. Bright Hawaiian fashions glowed everywhere. Some people, both men and women, wore flower leis.

Feeling paler, tenser, more rumpled and out of place than ever, Josie looked around the airport in concern. She had phoned Whitewater's hotel again, leaving word of when her plane was coming in, but she had no way of knowing if he would bother to meet her. She squared her shoulders. She would get her luggage, rent a car, find an inexpensive hotel, then leave another message for him.

She started to follow the signs that led toward the luggage carousel. She had just passed a vendor selling leis and orchids when she felt a strong hand grip her elbow and effortlessly turn her around. She looked up into the black-brown eyes of Aaron Whitewater. The high cheekbones were as handsome and exotic as she remembered, the mouth just as confident and irreverent. A lock of black-brown hair fell over one straight brow. He smiled carelessly. It was a disarming and yet dangerous smile.

"Aloha," he said with a smirk, and put a delicate lei of lavender orchids and pink buds over her head. Then, before she had yet recovered from the mere sight of him, he took her face between his large hands, tilted it up toward his, lowered his mouth to hers and kissed her.

His hands felt warm and vibrant against her pale cheeks, and his body, so near hers, seemed like a conduit for a giant jolt of energy into her weakened system. If she had felt like a ghost on the plane, she was suddenly startled back into warm and tingling life.

His mouth took sure and complete possession of hers, the subtle movement of his well-shaped lips teasing hers into new awareness. *Go ahead,* she thought, slightly dizzy, *kiss me, Whitewater. It's all right, because you're going to save Moon Flower. You're going to save everything.*

But as soon as she had rationalized his presumptuous kiss, he ended it. "Excuse that," he said, shrugging. "Just a local custom. Welcome to the Islands. Or, I guess in your case, the first set of islands."

He reached over and took her battered carryon bag from her. "I've got a place for you at my hotel. Let's grab your luggage and go. You can get out of that hot suit and into a cold gin fizz."

"Sounds good," she said, smiling up at him weakly. She could smell the faint fragrance of the lei, feel the sunny warmth of Hawaii even though they were still inside the airport. Aaron Whitewater had on crumpled khaki safari shorts and an ivory-colored Hawaiian shirt with black flowers printed on it.

She stood beside him in awkward silence as she waited for her luggage to appear. Her reaction to him last year had been no fluke. He made her feel distinctly odd all over. Not only that, he did what few men in her life had ever been able to do: he made her feel protected, even as he seemed to menace her in some primeval way. She didn't know what to say to him. She didn't know how she was going to begin to explain the mess about Bettina and Moon Flower and Lucas to him. She simply stood straighter, clutching her purse more tightly, feeling more tongue-tied by the minute.

He leaned down, putting his mouth so close to her ear that the warmth of his face seemed to burn her skin. "Do you want to tell me what kind of trouble you're in now? Or later. Over a drink."

Fatigue and befuddlement fell away from her, replaced by wariness. She stared up at him, eyes apprehensive. "I never said I was in trouble," she replied, her voice slightly choked. "Not in so many words."

He folded his arms across his chest. He glanced down at her coolly. "You're in trouble, all right. Big trouble. *Wasichu*—as my granddad used to say. More than can be counted, I'd guess."

She continued to stare up at him, her mouth slightly open. She tried to keep her chin from trembling. "How can you be so sure?" she asked.

He leaned close to her again. "I used a great power I have," he intoned mysteriously. "The name I give to this power," he said, tapping his forehead, "is logic. I know something has to be seriously amiss. What else could reduce you to saying you want me? Nothing else, right?"

"Right," Josie replied defensively, and hoped that she was telling the truth.

"Ah," he said, smiling almost to himself. "This could get interesting."

"So YOU LET SOMEBODY make off with your panda," he said ironically. "You're in big trouble, all right."

They sat at a glass table on the patio of Whitewater's hotel. Evening was falling fast, and Diamond Head was dusky in the distance. The waves rolled in to the beach in long blue and white curls. Plump dark doves bobbed about the patio tiles, in search of crumbs. The breeze stirred the small orchids growing behind Aaron Whitewater's chair.

Josie looked at him over the rim of her drink with resentment. "I didn't *let* anybody make off with her," she stated emphatically. "A crime was committed in the dead of night. If I'd known what was happening, I'd have given my life to stop it."

He tossed her a dark-eyed glance that seemed to cut through all her defenses and see directly into the secret center of her soul. "That's a strong statement," he observed in his husky voice. "You care that much about the animal?"

"Yes!" Josie returned passionately. "I do. I'm just grateful they didn't take Nan Wu, too."

"Two would probably be more than they could handle," he observed calmly. "And is that all you care about so deeply? These...creatures of yours?"

Josie tried to meet his black eyes without flinching. "They're not my creatures. They belong to the zoo. But in a sense they belong to everybody. They belong to the whole world, and that's why it's so wrong for one to be stolen, to be used like this. And yes, I guess that is all I care about—not just Moon Flower, but all the 'creatures' like her that are endangered, that have to be saved."

Aaron Whitewater's upper lip curled satirically at the corner. "Quite the high-minded little protectress, aren't you? The noble champion. The selfless savior. I'd recommend a suit of white armor—except it'd hide that pretty, leggy body. But that wouldn't bother you, would it? High-minded women like to forget they have bodies."

Tired and uneasy as Josie was, she bridled. "I've had more important things to think about," she retorted.

"And I never knew there was anything wrong with being high-minded. Or wanting to preserve animals—instead of hunting them like you."

The white beach gleamed silver under the rising moon, and music was floating from the hotel's western terrace. Whitewater sipped his mai tai and regarded her with disconcerting thoroughness. "Easy," he warned mildly, but there was steel in his voice. "You need me, remember?"

She sighed, leaning against the caned back of her chair. She stared at the sapphire-and-platinum sky and the palms silhouetted against it. "Yes," she admitted with reluctance. "I need you.

"My love," he answered with mock solemnity, "you need me in ways you don't even know yet."

Perplexed, Josie closed her eyes. Her tired body prickled with an unaccustomed warmth that had nothing to do with the balminess of the evening breeze. "Are you going to help me or not?" she asked.

She was not surprised when his answer was silence. She heard the drifting music, the breeze in the palms, the great purr of the surf.

"I'll help you," he answered at last, "for the panda's sake. Hunters are some of the most dedicated conservationists you've got, you know. And for your sister's sake, too. I'm beginning to see how she got into this mess. You're a tough act to follow, Saint Josephine. And I have the feeling you care more about the panda than the girl."

Josie's eyes flew open. "First," she replied, keeping her tone dangerously even, "don't ever call me Josephine. I hate it. And don't ever imply I'm not concerned about my sister. I'm scared sick about her."

"All right, Josie," he said, but he didn't sound chastened in the least. "But don't fret. If she cooperates and we get the panda back, and she's willing to turn state's evidence against Lucas, she'll probably get off with a slap on the wrist."

Josie found his words comforting, although she hated admitting it. "You have a law degree, too, I suppose?" she asked, trying to sound unimpressed.

"No," he returned, his tone as cool as her own. "My brother has the law degree. I have to rely on common sense. And common sense tells me we're going to have to work fast. We don't have that much time to find them. Kali Chenshan is a big island, and all of it is rough country. Beautiful, but rough. So common sense also tells me it's time to put you to bed. Please note that I said put you to bed, not take you to bed, so you can relax—for now. You need rest. Because what you're about to try would be, under most circumstances, just about impossible."

Josie finished her drink. She stared across the moonsilvered darkness at him. Her situation was difficult enough, and she wished he wouldn't keep complicating it with sexual innuendo. He made her nerves want to beg for mercy. "Impossible?" she asked bitterly. "Thanks for the encouragement. I need all I can get."

"Somewhere in the mountains are a panda and a couple of crazy mixed-up kids. You've not only got to find them, you've got to get your sister and the animal back to civilization—before Lucas does anything rash. And Lucas sounds like a guy who was born to be rash. He's like Kali Chenshan itself—volcanic. But at least you've got an advantage."

She looked at him questioningly. The moonlight gleamed on his dark hair, his high cheekbones, the proud planes of his face. "*I* have an advantage?" she asked with doubt.

"Just one, Saint Josie," he answered, raising his glass to her. "Me. Whitewater. And don't forget it."

She stood up. She picked up her purse. "I doubt," she said tartly, "that you'll let me forget it for a moment, Mr. Whitewater. I doubt you'll let me forget it for a single second. And what, by the way, are you going to charge me for the wonderful advantage of your expertise?"

He stood, looming over her. He put his forefinger beneath her chin, tipping her face up to his. "I haven't decided yet," he answered. "But I'll warn you, Josie. I'm not cheap. I'm about as expensive as you can get."

Again she was aware of the enormous power and energy of his tall body. Vitality radiated from him. Her heart seemed to slow, beating to the hypnotic rhythm of the surf. She drew in her breath sharply as his thumb lightly traced the pale curve of her jaw. "I guess I don't have any choice, do I?" she asked with more carelessness than she felt.

"No," he said, smiling down at her with satisfaction. "You don't."

The night wind stirred the dark fiery tumble of her curls. His face was hidden by the shifting shadows and she could feel his smile rather than see it. She stood tautly, conscious that the gentle touch of his hand upon her face seemed both a warning and a promise.

He let his hand fall away. He nodded in the direction of the hotel. "Get to bed, Josie," he said in his quietly gruff voice. He walked with her, but he didn't touch her again. Behind them, the ocean sang its ancient song in the moonlight and the darkness.

"How do you know," he challenged, as he walked her to the elevators, "that somebody wasn't listening in on our little telephone conversation last night? Doesn't that bother you?"

He pushed a button and an elevator door sighed open almost immediately. Josie stepped inside. Whitewater did not. She glanced at him. "If they knew, they probably would have stopped me," she said coolly.

"You're taking a big chance," he said, his mouth crooking slightly.

"Maybe I'm not afraid of taking chances," she replied, tossing her head. She punched the button to close the door.

He stood there smiling as the door began to slide shut.

"Maybe you should be. Afraid of taking chances."

"I know," she said tersely. She was grateful when the door cut off the sight of his mocking face.

But she had heard a note of genuine warning in his voice.

CHAPTER THREE

"WHAT DO YOU KNOW about the Kali Yins?"
Whitewater asked her. They were up early for breakfast at the outdoor dining room, and few of the hotel's
other guests had yet risen. The edge of the sky had
turned a tender turquoise, and the restless sea was sapphire, trimmed with the faintest gold.

"Not much," Josie admitted, liberally applying pa-
paya jam to her popover. "Mostly about the wildlife.
Several kinds of birds are unique to the Kali Yins, also
the nikinikis, a kind of deer. They're very rare."

He eyed her dubiously. He obviously didn't find her
knowledge practical.

If Aaron Whitewater had looked casual enough to be
a son of the Islands yesterday, today he looked strictly
business, and grim business at that. He wore heavy
boots and jungle fatigue pants that seemed to have
about twenty pockets. His long-sleeved khaki shirt was
rolled up to his elbows, exposing the tanned and sin-
ewy strength of his forearms. His khaki bush vest
seemed to contain another dozen or so pockets, and his
cotton bush hat, one side snapped up, rested on the table beside the silver coffeepot.

He reached into the back compartment of his vest
and drew out a map, which he unfolded on the double
linen tablecloths, beside the Swiss crystal and English
silverware.

When Josie had come downstairs for breakfast, she had felt self-conscious in her wheat-colored denims, blue-green turtleneck and high leather boots. She'd fancied herself dressed for combat in a world where everyone else was garbed for a beach party. Now, looking at Whitewater, she wondered if she had begun to understand the difficulty of what they were about to attempt.

"Look," he said, taking a pen from one of his myriad pockets and pointing to an island shaped like a scallop shell. The rising sun glinted on his brown-black hair. "This is Kali Chenshan. It's my guess Lucas took your panda here. Kali Yushan would have been better, but he'd really have to rough it there. I have the feeling he's the kind of boy who doesn't like to rough it, that he's a coward at heart."

Josie nodded solemnly. Lucas had always struck her as full of false and self-dramatizing bravado. She sipped her coffee and waited for Whitewater to tell her exactly where they were going.

The dark-eyed glance he gave her was as formidably businesslike as his general air. "The Kali Yins are a peculiar bunch of islands," he informed her. The set of his bronzed face made it clear she was to remember everything he said.

"They were too rugged to be considered good for much when Captain Cook discovered them in the eighteenth century. Their ownership was disputed until they became a United States protectorate in 1945. A few rich men and corporations have tried to make money off them. They've failed. The Kali Yins produce a little tapa, a little sugar, a little pineapple, but mostly they've just got scenery. The tourists haven't discovered them yet, and with the competition from Hawaii, which is more developed, it may be a while—thank God—before they're exploited."

He paused and without ceremony poured Josie more coffee. "In the 1960s," he continued, "the Trans-Pacific Foods Corporation got the bright idea of trying coffee plantations on the Kali Yins. They picked Kali Chenshan and the smallest island, Rana Pula. Coffee's grown successfully at Kona, here in Hawaii. They figured the conditions in the Kali Yins were even better—and a coffee tree doesn't mind a mountainside."

Josie was setting down her coffee cup, but Whitewater's large hand folded momentarily around her slender one. Once more she was startled to feel the strength and vitality that emanated from him. He reminded her of the big black and golden male tigers in the zoo, which even at rest had an aura of natural power.

"This coffee," he murmured, nodding at the fragile cup in her hand, "isn't island coffee. It's shipped in. The big coffee industry never got off the ground in the Kali Yins. In the 1970s some kind of blight hit, a plague almost. Trans-Pacific almost lost its corporate shirt. To make sure the blight didn't spread, they had to burn their fields. Then Kana-Puma, the central volcano on Kali Chenshan, started acting up. Trans-Pacific decided the old legend of native curses was true. They got the hell out."

He had released her hand, but it still tingled from his touch. She tried to pretend his casual contact didn't affect her. "So what," she asked with assumed calm, "does coffee have to do with pandas?"

He gave her a sharp look. "This," he growled between his teeth. He drew three circles on the map of the island. "These are the sites of the headquarters of the three main plantations on Chenshan. The fields were burned. But the buildings are still standing—or most of them. Number one is still accessible by road. I don't think your friend Lucas would like that. Plus, the area's been taken over by local tapa and cane farmers—too many people.''

He pointed to a second circle. ''This is the second headquarters. But it's too close to Kana-Puma, the volcano, and the fire pits still act up from time to time. It's high, it's isolated, but it's dangerous. I don't think your friend wants to go there, either.''

Josie looked at him with new respect. So far his logic was irrefutable. She pointed to the third circle, inked in an area called the Mala Lui Valley, ''You mean—'' she breathed ''—you think Lucas has Bettina and Moon Flower there? At the third plantation site?''

He met her gaze, his own unreadable. ''Right.''

She set her jaw. She started to push her chair back from the table. She threw down her white napkin. ''Then let's go,'' she said.

Once more he reached across the table. He grasped her wrist. Somehow he managed to exert enough force to keep her in her chair yet not hurt her in the slightest. ''Not yet,'' he said quietly. He allowed his hand to remain circled around her wrist for the length of the pause between two beats of the surf. ''You don't understand everything yet. Drink your coffee. Have some more breakfast. Enjoy civilization while you can. Because we're about to get primitive, Saint Josie. Very primitive.''

He released her hand and leaned back in his chair. He stared out at the white beach and the blue waves, at the gulls dipping and winging over the breakers. ''Trans-Pacific put this third plantation in one of the most spectacular—but inaccessible—parts of the island. It was going to be their showplace. It's marked as a valley on the map, but it's really more of a gorge, a tremendous canyon with mountains and forests in it. The plantation is on top of Ra-Koma—the Mount of Cloudy Gods. Nobody lived there before Trans-Pacific tried it. And nobody's lived there since—nobody on the right side of the law, anyway. There are only two ways to get there. A volcanic eruption covered the company road. But there's still a landing strip—in bad shape, but you can get in by air, which I'm sure Lucas did. Or you can get there by foot. That's how we're going to have to go. Unless we want to announce to him that we're coming in.''

Josie swallowed hard. She stared at the doves that strutted from table to table, begging crumbs of toast and popovers. She stared at the Swiss crystal and English silver on the table, and then at the orchids growing next to their table. Then she looked at the big man, half Sioux Indian, who sat across from her. Again she had the eerie feeling he could see into her soul.

She shrugged uneasily. ''I can walk,'' she replied at last. ''I've climbed mountains before, too. I've done a lot of those things with my father. And I'm in good shape.''

''I can see that,'' he said, and for the first time that morning, the familiar smile played about his sculpted lips. ''I saw that from the first.''

Suddenly Josie laughed. She threw back her head, shut her eyes and giggled helplessly. The waves played their muffled, primeval rhythm, silver and crystal clinked lightly in the background, and she felt the morning sun warm her face.

"Good Lord," muttered Whitewater in disgust. "Don't tell me you're hysterical already."

She opened her eyes, giving another little gasp of laughter. Whitewater scowled slightly at her. Behind him, the sky was now perfectly blue. The waves mirrored it and caught the silvery rays of the sun.

"I'm sorry," she said, wiping a trace of a tear from her eye. She ran her hand ineffectually over her red-brown curls. "Last week my biggest worry was wondering if my car would be frozen. It was seven below zero with a windchill factor of twenty-five below. I was in a nice safe zoo in the middle of the city in the middle of the country in the middle of winter, and now . . ."

She gestured helplessly, trying to take in the sunshine, the surf, the orchids, the doves, the crumpled map on the table between them.

"Glad you can retain your sense of humor," he said out of the side of his mouth. "But remember this. I can't let you slow me down. I can't leave you behind, either. You're the one who has to care for the panda once we find her—understand that? You've got to keep up with me. Everything depends on it. And I can't take it easy on you."

Josie's fit of frivolity vanished. She knew that Whitewater wasn't trying to frighten her. He was telling her the truth. The hard, unvarnished truth. "I can keep up with you," she answered, her head high. And she would, because she had to, for Moon Flower and for Bettina.

"We'll see," he answered, one straight brow rising dubiously. "You're also going to have to do as I say—exactly—every step of the way. You take orders, you don't ask questions, you *obey*. Understand? I may be just the hired help to you, but my job is to keep you alive, and get the panda and your sister back alive, too. Got it?''

Josie didn't like his commanding tone, but nodded briskly. ''I've got it,'' she bit off. ''Aye, aye, captain. You say it, I do it.''

''Good.'' He nodded, and in the morning light his eyes seemed black and relentless as obsidian. ''We'll see about that, too. And one more thing, Josie. This is what everything else rests on, so understand this best of all. You've got to trust me—more than you trust yourself. In a sense, you have to belong to me completely. You have to trust me with your life.''

A dove hopped boldly onto their table, cocked a black and greedy eye at the bread basket. From somewhere, a tiny lavender orchid detached itself and fluttered down to rest on Josie's empty plate, beside a dab of jam. Once again, nothing seemed quite real.

Only Aaron Whitewater, as implacable and solid as Diamond Head on the horizon, seemed to have reality. She looked at his sun-burnished face, his mysterious dark eyes, his brown-black hair stirring in the morning breeze. ''I trust you,'' she breathed softly.

For a long moment his answer seemed to be silence. He studied her dark red curls glinting so fiercely in the sun, the determined aquamarine of her eyes, the constellation of freckles on her pale face. ''Good,'' he said gruffly. ''Now. Let's go.''

Like a good soldier, she rose immediately. But some frightened and rebellious part of her mind was already asking questions and fomenting trouble. *What if he's wrong?* asked that forbidden sector of her thoughts. *He's only guessing, after all. What if he's just flat-out dead wrong about where they are? What then? What*

*happens to Moon Flower? What becomes of the baby?
And my sister?*

He must have read her thoughts. His eyes locked with
hers again in hypnotic challenge. "Trust me," he ordered.

Except she was sure he hadn't opened his lips. It was
as if the thought sprang, strong and defiant, directly
from his mind to her own. And she understood.

THREE HOURS LATER the pilot of their small hired plane
set the craft down with a thump on the narrow tarmac
of Kali Chenshan's little airport.

Wordlessly, Whitewater and the pilot unloaded their
gear. Whitewater had already proved to be a hard task-
master. After all the years of traveling with her father,
Josie had thought she could pack for an outing. Aaron
Whitewater had thought otherwise.

He unpacked everything, casting aside her sleeping
bag, air mattress and pillow in favor of a simple ground
cloth and army blanket of his own. He gave a snort of
barely disguised derision at her changes of lacy underwear, but allowed her to keep them. He cut her other
supplies down to an extra shirt, extra jeans, several
changes of socks and her ancient leather cardigan.

She had to keep her medical supplies for Moon
Flower, and she insisted on keeping her small makeup
case. He grimaced, but finally agreed to the latter.
"You've got to carry all this stuff on your back, you
know," he cautioned dryly. "About halfway up some
three-thousand-foot mountain, that makeup case is
going to feel as heavy as a brick."

"I'll throw it away when that happens, not before,"
Josie returned stubbornly. To her surprise, he objected
no further.

She in turn kept her disapproving silence when she saw his arsenal. He was taking a machete and a rifle in a leather-and-canvas case. The rifle made Josie nervous. She abhorred violence and from the beginning had thought to get Moon Flower back without it.

Whitewater saw her nervous reaction. "We're going into the forest, dammit," he said darkly. "What am I supposed to do if we're charged by a wild boar? Offer it a cookie?"

He pulled the skimpy gear, the rifle and a small backpack of supplies into the back of a rented Jeep. Wordlessly he gestured for Josie to get in.

"Where are we going?" she asked, looking about uneasily. Chenshan's shoreline was a forbidding one, with high dark cliffs against which the sea crashed wildly. Inland, the first ring of mountains rose, dramatic and darkly green against the brilliant sky.

"To Horace Coelho's. He's a Hawaiian who runs a small ranch up in the mountains. But more important, he outfits hunting and freshwater fishing expeditions."

Josie clamped a protective hand on her straw hat to keep it in place. "You mean we're going to get more gear?" she asked hopefully, as the Jeep bucked into life and headed toward the mountains.

He gave her one of his stony-faced derisive glances. "We've got too much gear now, to my mind. I wouldn't go in with anything except the rifle, ropes and medical supplies, if I had my way. But I have to keep you in luxury and comfort."

"Luxury and comfort?" Josie protested, thinking of the two slim bedrolls and the knapsack, which as far as she knew, held nothing but freeze-dried gruel and protein tablets. "If we're not going to get a tent or something, why are we going to this Horace—Horace..."

"Horace Coelho's," he supplied. "For horses. You are able to ride a horse, aren't you, Miss Perfection?"

"Of course," murmured Josie, hopeful once more. "You mean we can take horses to the plantation site? That would be a big help—"

"We can take them in the first fifteen miles. We'll get Horace's son to go with us. Then he'll take them back. After that, we're on our own."

Josie looked at the sheer height of the mountains visible from the steep road. The landscape looked as if some giant had taken the native lava in his mighty hand and squeezed it until sharp and massive ridges arose between his great fingers. Greenery cloaked the jagged peaks like dark velvet.

"This is all . . . quite impressive," Josie said lamely, but in her heart she wondered how they would ever conquer such steeps.

"Impressive?" He laughed mockingly. "This is nothing, yet. Wait till you see the *real* mountains."

The *real* mountains? Josie wondered with sinking heart, looking at the looming green peaks. She glanced at Whitewater, who was concentrating on negotiating the hairpin curves of the narrow road. He looked no more concerned than a commuter driving to his daily office job. Except, she thought uncomfortably, few commuters were this large, bronzed and muscular, or filled with such daunting power.

She tried to concentrate on remembering Moon Flower's beloved round face with its black ears and bandit's mask. And she tried, for the thousandth time, to forgive her sister.

Horace Coelho was a good-natured, handsome brown-faced man with a good-natured, handsome brown-faced son, Berke. But for all their geniality both

Coelho's shared the admirable trait of asking no questions, although they cheerfully answered those put to them.

No, nobody had mentioned any suspicious mainlanders in the village. It was winter on the mainland, and Kali Chenshan was drawing a few more sightseers than usual, sometimes up to a dozen or more a day, but no one had stood out.

Yes, there had been rumors of a plane in the Mala Lui Valley, around Ra-Koma, the Mount of Cloudy Gods. But then there were always rumors of planes gliding in at dawn or dusk, on mysterious errands that were best left unexamined.

Yes, the volcano, Kana-Puma, had been quiet lately, although one of the fire pits flared up from time to time. The volcano scientists said no danger was imminent. But what did they know for sure? Was not Kana-Puma where the island's chief ancient deity, counterpart of Pele, the Hawaiian volcano goddess, lived? And, asked Horace Coelho with nervous reverence, what mere mortal could predict what a force as powerful as Kana-Puma might do?

Yes, said Horace in the same uneasy tone, local people who were wise stayed away from Ra-Koma, the Mount of Cloudy Gods. Such places had been made remote from humankind for a reason. It was *pilikia*—trouble—for the race of men to challenge the Cloudy Gods.

"Bad medicine," Whitewater muttered, lapsing into memories of his Sioux grandfather. But Horace did not object when Whitewater said that he and Josie were heading in that general direction. "She's a birdwatcher," Whitewater lied smoothly, nodding toward

Josie. "She wants to see the rainbow doves, the hermit geese."

"Ah," said Horace Coelho wisely, resting his twinkling dark eyes on Josie. "You have selected your guide wisely. This one, Whitewater, is the *kahuna* of outdoorsmen. The expert, the one of strange powers. I mean no insult when I say it is sometimes hard to believe he is *hapa haole*—part white."

Whitewater's face was at first unreadable, but then he gave Horace his wry half smile. He refused the older man's invitation to stay for lunch; he wanted to be off immediately. Would Berke take them with the horses as far as they could go, and could Donald and Daniel, Horace's teenage twin sons, take the Jeep back to the village?

"Consider yourself started, consider the Jeep returned," the genial Horace said with a nod. Then he insisted on sending food with them, to eat when they finally dismounted.

Josie's mount was a dark sorrel gelding that Horace joked almost matched her curls. Whitewater swung expertly into the saddle of a horse he had obviously ridden before, a great brown-black stallion named Holo. Berke Coelho fell in beside Whitewater on his compact ivory-colored gelding, Netsuke.

Josie followed the two, keeping silent as they took to the narrow trail leading farther into the interior of the island. From time to time the men chatted easily, ignoring her. She stayed quiet, knowing that Whitewater wanted no word of their business on the island leaking out, even to such trusted friends as the Coelhos.

She concentrated on riding techniques as her surefooted horse, Keone, made his way steadily up the rising path. The weather in Chenshan forests was crisper

than on the Honolulu beach, and Josie was glad that
Whitewater had made her pull a long-sleeved cotton
sweater over her turquoise turtleneck.

The forests here were a mixture of pines as well as
palms and ferns. The higher they climbed, the more
frequently thick groves of bamboo appeared, and the
shiny leaves of the wild ginger plants glittered in the filtered sunlight.

Soon the pink, white and yellow of the small wild
orchids gave way to the strange scarlet puffball flowers
of the ohia lehua trees. The hibiscus shrubs were fewer,
their lacy coral petals smaller.

The air grew cooler, even misty, as the three as-
cended. Josie's mount was more careful about where he
placed his hooves, for the path was growing narrower,
more humped by roots and netted by creepers. Josie had
to duck frequently, taking shelter behind Keone's neck
from overhanging branches and vines.

Whitewater and Berke had stopped talking, concentrating on the more serious task of picking their way
over the trail. Whitewater let Berke go first, who slashed
the unfriendliest overhanging vegetation with his
machete. Whitewater said nothing at all to Josie, but
from time to time he glanced back over his shoulder, his
black eyes measuring her from beneath the canvas brim
of his hat.

He looked like Indiana Jones, Josie thought wryly,
as she scrubbed a spot on her cheek where a branch of
an ohia lehua had impertinently slapped. He looked as
if he were enjoying every minute of this. And expected
her to give up any time now.

She was hungry, her stomach growling slightly, and
her bottom was sore from the saddle and her thighs
ached. But she refused to give Whitewater the satisfac-

tion of hearing her complain. She stayed as resolutely silent as he.

Although the overhanging trees hid the sky, Josie could tell the sun was going down when they finally dismounted. The trail, steep before, seemed almost vertical, and so narrow that it appeared little more than a trail for wild animals.

Stiffly Josie swung down from the back of the gentle Keone and gave him an affectionate scratch behind his ears. Against her will she let Whitewater help her fasten her bedroll in place on her shoulders, for he used some sort of system she didn't know. His lithe, powerful hands moving so surely against her shoulder blades made her shiver with a chill deeper than that of the approaching evening cool.

They bade Berke goodbye. He flashed them a white smile of well-wishing, but Josie could see troubled puzzlement in his dark eyes. She didn't think he believed Whitewater's glib lie about bird-watching, but he was too much the gentleman to say otherwise.

As Berke rode away from them through the thickening shadows, Josie felt her heart tighten with apprehension. The man and the three horses disappeared quickly into the undergrowth. The last thing she saw was the dim reddish flash of Keone's switching tail.

She and Whitewater were alone in the forests of the Mala Lui Valley.

Somewhere a kiki bird whistled and another answered it. The fateful sound—the almost comical *tweety-po-wit* reminded her of the lost Moon Flower and the wayward Bettina. Two days ago at this time she had been driving home through the Chicago snow. Now she stood alone beside the towering height of Aaron Whitewater in this semitropical jungle.

She swallowed hard and straightened her shoulders under the burden of the bedroll. "What now?" she asked, looking up at him. She was starving and all of her muscles were starting to hurt.

He returned her questioning stare with one of maddening impassiveness. "Now we go up," he stated, jerking a thumb in the direction of the treacherous-looking path.

Josie's head swam slightly at the prospect. She would have fallen on her knees in thanks if he had said, "We'll eat and then get some sleep—and surprise, I really brought your air mattress, after all." Instead she nodded stoically.

"Up," she repeated, keeping all emotion from her voice.

Whitewater led the way. "Don't depend on handholds," he warned over his shoulder. "Always be sure you've got a good foothold in a situation like this."

"Certainly," Josie sniffed, but at that very moment a vine she had grabbed for leverage gave way, and she almost tumbled backward. Whitewater's sure hand shot out and grabbed her clutching one. Almost effortlessly he pulled her back into place and waited for her to find a dependable foothold.

"Watch where I step," he ordered shortly, and turned back to climbing.

Josie resisted the desire to make a face behind his back and instead focused her attention on where he set his feet. She tried to follow exactly in his footsteps, but could not, for his legs were much longer than hers. Frequently he had to turn back, extend his hand and fairly hoist her to the next firm spot. Each time his hand touched hers, it seemed as if she grasped a lightning bolt that sent his special brand of energy surging restlessly through her body.

"How much farther are we going?" she finally panted after he had taken her in hand for the fifth time and hauled her to relative safety.

"We'll go another half hour, maybe, forty-five minutes," he answered curtly. "As long as there's light. There's a waterfall up here I want to get to. We'll need water."

We'll need water, Josie wanted to mock evilly at his broad back. As if she didn't know. She almost slipped again, but once again his hand was there to catch her, hold her, bear her upward.

It was a particularly difficult section of trail, and he kept a tight hold on her as he fought their way up the incline. Josie tried to keep from dwelling on how far up they might be and how firmly and warmly Whitewater's hand seemed welded to her own.

"How's Berke going to get back to the ranch before dark?" she asked. She was breathless and tried to keep from panting the question.

"He won't. He'll sleep by the trail and make it back tomorrow morning," Aaron muttered. He turned and lifted her bodily above him, his hands almost spanning her waist. "Put your foot on that rock," he ordered. "And save your breath. We're climbing a mountain. Why do you keep wanting to talk, woman?"

Josie obeyed, glad when his hands released her and he inched his way past her to lead the way once more. Her heart thudded maniacally in her chest. Her breath seemed to have deserted her.

She concentrated on climbing and tried not to think of the man she was climbing with. She moved with blind determination, reminding herself that each difficult step took her closer to Moon Flower, in all her beautiful innocence—and Bettina, in all her guilt.

Mercifully Whitewater stopped just as the shadows seemed about to overwhelm the forest. Even in the dim light Josie could see the tall crystal cascade of the waterfall. High, regal and almost delicate-looking, it splashed and foamed into a waiting pool that fed a wide brook.

"We'll stop here," Whitewater announced, measuring the clearing with a hawkish gaze. Gratefully Josie relaxed, but only momentarily, for once again she had to suffer the hot pricky sensations created by his expert hands unfastening the bedroll from her back. She sank gratefully onto a nearby stone and sat, rubbing her shoulders.

Without comment, he unfastened his own bedroll and knapsack. He moved quietly into the underbrush, gathering a huge pile of ferns, which he spread in a mossy spot of earth not far from the pool. He unfolded his ground cloth so it covered half the heap of ferns. Josie realized she could either sleep next to him, sharing the softness of the ferns, or she could lie as best she could on the rocky earth. She was a naturalist, but she had no desire to crash through exotic shrubbery gathering fronds in the darkness.

She spread out her own ground cloth, and at Whitewater's orders, stowed her spare clothing and other supplies in the crook of a branch of a nearby ohia lehua tree to keep it from the dew. She had put on her leather cardigan and unrolled her blanket next to his, close enough to share the ferns but far enough, she hoped, to maintain some decorum.

She shivered slightly. In spite of the darkness he seemed to see the small movement. "I'm going to chance a fire," he said calmly. "But not a big one and not all night. Just for coffee."

Josie nodded, almost too tired to care. She listened to the restful splashing of the waterfall and wondered if she would be able to sleep. She had camped with her father often, but that had been luxury compared to the way Whitewater settled into nature. She watched as he gathered a few dry twigs and branches and quickly breathed fiery life into them.

Gratefully she drank the coffee he gave her and shared the food Horace Coelho had insisted they bring. There was Hawaiian jerked beef, banana muffins, mangoes and a kind of fish smoked with coconut husks. To Josie, every morsel was almost unbearably delicious, as only food eaten out-of-doors can be.

"That," muttered Whitewater, finishing his coffee, "really was your last taste of luxury. From here on in we rough it."

He put out the small fire. Somehow he made it disappear immediately and completely and darkness completely overtook the campsite. He stirred in the shadows, but Josie couldn't see him. The scudding clouds had hidden the few stars that had shone down on the clearing. Now that she was fed, Josie was fueled to worry once again. She prayed once more that Moon Flower was all right, that Bettina was somehow protecting her.

She heard Whitewater winding himself in his blanket. He seemed to be settling down for the night. She sat on her own blanket, her arms clasped around her bent knees. All day she had gone without speaking her fears, but she could no longer restrain herself.

"Aaron," she began carefully, using his given name in the hope of sounding friendly and uncritical.

"Call me Whitewater," he corrected without rancor. "I prefer it. Traditional. Name of my forefathers and all that."

"All right," she returned, her patience wearing thin. "Whitewater. We came most of this way by horseback and the rest of the way climbing straight up. Tomorrow I have the feeling we do more climbing. Lots more."

She paused, waiting for his answer. "Right," he said laconically. "We climb up. Then we climb down. Then we climb up some more. But you've got it. We climb."

"Fine," she said between clenched teeth. "And when we finally get to the top of Ra-ra whatever it is—"

"Ra-Koma," he supplied lazily. "The Mount of Cloudy Gods. A poetic lot, the natives of the Kali Yins."

"We get to the top of Ra-Koma," she continued relentlessly, "and suppose we even find Moon Flower, right there, just like you think we will, and we even get her without any trouble—" She stopped, the question implied in her voice.

"Well?" he asked, and yawned. "What?"

"Well," Josie replied sarcastically, "how do we get her back down. That's *what*. Or are you just going to throw 250 pounds of pregnant panda over your manly shoulder and climb back down for two or three days? Because if that's your plan, I don't think much of it."

"You're ridiculous," he observed calmly. "Think, will you?"

"I *have* been thinking," Josie retorted, staring into the darkness. "That's why I asked."

"We'll get her out the same way Lucas got her in. His plane," Whitewater said, disgust in his tone.

"But what if she's not even there?" Josie demanded, nervousness edging her voice. "We can't be sure, can we? I mean, all day I've been thinking, if the road to Ra-Koma's gone, then how did Lucas and Bettina get to the village when Bettina called? We might be in the wrong place altogether."

She could tell she was trying his patience. "They got to the village the same way they got to the mountain," he answered with exaggerated forbearance. "By plane, remember? I told you once—you have to trust me. I'm a hunter. I have to try to think like the prey. In this case the prey is Lucas, so I'm having to experiment with twisted thinking, which I don't much like. But what I'm doing is hunting, and hunting is my business. I'm starting it again first thing tomorrow morning, so will you be quiet and go to sleep? Now I know how the Sioux nation was defeated. You people sent out your redheads and they talked us to death."

"Very funny," Josie returned, but he didn't deign to answer. Soon the evenness of his breathing told her he had fallen asleep. She wrapped herself cocoonlike in her blanket. The ferns were more comfortable than she would have imagined, but she was restless.

She lay for a long time, listening to the low roar of the waterfall. No matter how tightly she wound the blanket around herself, she was still cold. She would manage to doze only to waken again, shivering. Mist had settled over them.

She stirred uncomfortably, her teeth chattering. She missed her pillow. She wanted another blanket. The night was endless. Her movements awoke Whitewater, who, she sensed somehow, was suddenly alert beside her.

She went still, trying not to shudder with the cold. He sighed deeply. "Your teeth," he said accusingly, "sound like maracas. Or castanets. Come here. I'll share my blanket."

"No," Josie answered in a small voice. "I don't want to."

He swore sleepily. "Yes, you do. Come here." One long arm stretched out and drew her next to him so swiftly she gasped. His arm was warm and bare, as was the wide chest she found herself pressed against. He started to reach for her blanket, to rearrange both coverings around them, when he stopped. She could feel his stare, rather than see it in the cool and pearly mist.

"You've got your clothes on," he said in a low voice.

"Of course," Josie replied, shivering in spite of his gift of warmth. "I'd be frozen solid if I didn't."

"You're practically frozen solid because you do," he growled. "Anybody knows you don't sleep in your clothes. They hold moisture. Get out of those things and come here."

"No!" Josie protested, but she did not try to scramble away from the heat of his body.

"I'm not going to do anything to you," he reproached her, disdain in his voice. "I told you before, do as I say and don't ask questions. Your survival depends on me. Now take those clothes off before you catch pneumonia, or I'll take them off for you. All of them."

Authority rumbled in his husky voice. She was suddenly glad for the curtain of mist around them. "All right, all right," she consented and wriggled swiftly from her clothes.

"Here," he demanded, and took her clothes from her. What he did with them, she had no idea. She shivered, unprotected in the chill that veiled the night. Then he was next to her again, wrapping the two blankets tightly about them.

She realized with a start that he, too, was completely unclothed. But the warmth of his body was transmitting itself to hers, heating her like a secret sun in the heart of the night. He was right. She was far warmer naked than she had been clad. Odd, she thought guiltily, this was a camping tip she'd never seen in the Girl Scout Handbook. As far as modesty went, it was sorely lacking, but in terms of warmth, it was wonderful.

Whitewater shifted his body so it curled more protectively around hers. His muscular arm was beneath her head, pillowing it comfortably. His breath fanned her throat like a private, caressing, summery breeze.

"Now," he ordered in a harsh whisper, "go to sleep, will you?" His large hand rested companionably on her bare waist.

Exhausted, but warmed at last, Josie sank against him, her eyes fluttering shut. He cradled her to him more intimately.

"Ah," he said unhappily in her ear. "The things a man has to do in the service of his country's pandas. Good night, Josie."

"Good night, Whitewater." She sighed blissfully, too tired to be embarrassed further by the intimacy of their closeness and nakedness.

She was asleep before she knew it.

Whitewater held her and stared for a long time up into the impenetrable mist that hid the stars. His grandfather had taught him many things, many secrets of the earth and of nature. But the old man hadn't warned him about a night like this. If the old man's spirit was out walking among the stars and looking down on his grandson now, what would he think?

He kissed the woman beside him on the delicate curve where her throat met her shoulder. The incredible smoothness of her skin felt like warm and fragrant silk beneath his lips. Then he sighed uncomfortably. And, at last, he slept.

CHAPTER FOUR

TWEETY-PO-WIT, sang the little black-and-white kiki bird. Josie awoke slowly, languidly, aware of the aroma of coffee, and fish frying. The ferns beneath her were feathery soft. The blankets around her were warm and heavy.

Half-opening her eyes, she saw the deep jade green of the forest and the bright feathery blooms of the scarlet ohia lehua blossoms. The patches of sky that shone through the leaves were the misty blue of middle dawn, streaked with pink. She felt curiously chilled and pulled the blankets tighter.

Good grief, I'm naked! She jerked the blankets tighter still, clutching them against her breasts. Her blue-green eyes shot open. She sat up, looking around wildly. It all came surging back: Bettina had betrayed her, Moon Flower was stolen, and Josie was somewhere in the Pacific, naked in the forest with Whitewater.

"Good morning," said a grinning Whitewater, studying her bewildered face. He knelt beside a tidy little fire, frying two large trout. "I let you sleep late. But don't get spoiled. We've got climbing to do."

The trout smelled wonderful, the coffee smelled divine, sent from heaven, but Josie's confusion overwhelmed all else. "Where are my clothes?" she asked in a small voice.

"Wrapped in your cardigan," he answered calmly, nodding at the leather sweater bundled into a crotch of a nearby screw pine. "You redheads can really blush. Impressive. Kind of like a chameleon."

"Do you...share your body heat with all your women customers?" she asked, blushing more furiously and trying to reach her clothes. "This meant nothing at all, you know, Whitewater."

He set the frying pan on a nearby stone and came to stand over her. He picked up the bundled cardigan and handed it to her, his long shadow falling over her. "It's a special service," he muttered dryly. "You'll pay extra for it. And don't worry. I know it doesn't mean anything. Get dressed and get up. Or do you want to loll around naked all day?"

To Josie he suddenly seemed dangerously tall, dangerously male and dangerously close. "I don't loll," she said, wriggling awkwardly beneath the blankets to don her clothes. She felt, rather than saw, him move away.

"On the other hand," he said from the camp fire, "why don't you take a nice shower under the waterfall before you dress? Gets the blood circulating. I won't look. I'm not that interested."

Josie paused. The thought of a cleansing, tingling shower was enticing. She peered out of the blankets again. True to his word, Whitewater was ignoring her. She rose carefully, holding the blankets around her, and hobbled to the other side of the waterfall, where she could bathe screened by the giant ferns and bamboo.

She dropped the blanket and stepped into the icy pool. She gasped with the pleasant sting of the cold. At the edge of the waterfall, droplets pelted down like a sheet of diamond rain. She stepped into that shower of diamonds and gasped again, throwing her head back.

When she emerged, she'd never felt cleaner. It almost seemed a shame to put clothing back on, but she did.

She took her boots back to the fire and sat on a rock, pulling them on. "Feel better?" Whitewater asked, with only a slight maliciousness in his smile.

Josie shook her head vigorously, making the last droplets fly away from her dark red curls. She was revived, whole again. This man would not bait or irritate her.

"Where'd you get the fish?" she asked, helping herself to the coffee.

"Speared them," he replied, using his Swiss army knife to pick one up and set it in a metal mess kit dish for her. He reached into one of his innumerable pockets and handed her some sort of contrivance that unfolded into both a fork and spoon.

Josie ate the crisp trout hungrily. "You really are the great white hunter, aren't you?" she asked saucily, but she saw the smile freeze on his handsome face.

"Wrong choice of words," he returned after an interminable pause. "The great half-breed hunter is more like it."

She fought to keep another blush from coloring her face. "I'm sorry," she said, then added with her usual frankness, "I didn't know it bothered you. I mean, what difference does it make, your being part Sioux?"

"It makes no difference," he said curtly, "now." He poured her the last of the coffee. He stared into the flames of the fire.

"Meaning it did once?" Josie probed. His face looked so controlled and mysterious under the brim of his hat that she longed to know what secrets he kept so well to himself.

He shrugged, got up and filled the coffeepot with water. He threw it on the fire so that the coals were sodden and steaming. "Once it did. When I was a kid. I'm not a kid anymore," he muttered.

Indeed you're not, she thought. *You're quite a man, Aaron Whitewater. But who are you, really?*

"Tell me about your parents," she said, forging on with typical boldness. "About yourself."

"They fell in love," he answered curtly, eyeing her darkly. "Then they fell out of love. I grew up with my grandfather. At the Rosebud Reservation. My Aunt Cora had saved her money. She offered to put my brother and me through college. I said I'd rather she'd loan me enough to buy in with a hunting outfitter. I'd worked through high school as a guide. She did. I did. I was good at what I do. Now here we are. End of life story."

The brusqueness of his manner told Josie not to ask further. He clearly didn't like talking about his past. The sarcastically delivered summary was all she was likely to get from him.

She watched as he expertly gathered their things together, cleaned the utensils, and rerolled the blankets. She stood so he could fasten her bedroll to her shoulders again. Once more she was altogether too conscious of his fingers moving so deftly across her back.

She peered up at his stony face from under the straw brim of her hat. Her heart skipped slightly. "It's too bad," she said softly, "that you like to kill things."

He gave the fastening of the bedroll a final jerk, which hurt slightly and made her stand straighter. "I don't like to kill things," he returned, his smile snide. "I like to hunt them. There's a difference."

"Not that I can see," she answered, uncomfortable beneath his cool black gaze.

"No," he answered, irony in his voice, "you can't. That's your problem. Come on. That trail keeps going up."

THE TRAIL WENT UP and up, it seemed to Josie. The morning was a repeat of the evening before, but far worse. It seemed Whitewater spent half his time pulling her behind him or lifting her ahead of him. On one particularly terrifying steep, he roped her to him, so that if she fell, he could dig in and save her.

Once he had to tie her to him and swing the two of them across a small chasm. Josie had been blind with fear, and clung to him desperately. On they climbed. Nothing seemed to faze him, and nothing seemed able to stop him. She managed to stumble on, as if caught in the wake of some remarkably powerful force. And more than once in the course of the morning, she trusted her life to him.

By the time they reached the summit of the first mountain, the day had become a sun-dappled nightmare for Josie. The imperative that ruled her every breath was to keep going up. She hurt everywhere, but most of the time she was too awed and frightened to notice. In the unending bad dream of that climb, there was one dependable reality that promised safety and always delivered it. Whitewater.

When they reached the top, even he was panting. "We'll stop here," he said raggedly. "You need to eat."

She nodded dumbly. She made her way to a fallen log and sank onto it. She buried her face in her aching hands. They had made it. They were at the top. She wanted to sob with relief. *I'm coming, Moon Flower,* she thought wearily. *I'm coming, baby. Hang on.* Then, *Bettina, I don't know if I can ever forgive you.*

While she sat, too overwhelmed to even move, Whitewater built one of his small, neat fires. He cooked some sort of dried vegetable soup, made coffee and cut off pieces of jerky for the two of them. He had to force Josie to eat.

She chewed tiredly, and he looked at her with concern. "You're not giving out on me?" he asked, raising one dark brow in speculation.

She shook her head. "I'm fine," she said hoarsely.

He came and sat on the ground before her. "Let's see those hands," he ordered. "We've got to take care of them."

Numbly she showed him her punished hands. "Got some cuts," he observed, taking her hands between his large ones. "We have to clean them up. We want to get down by tonight. There's a grotto down there where we can stay."

"What?" Josie asked stupidly, staring at him. Under the shadow of his hat brim his eyes looked dark and unyielding. "What?" she repeated. For the first time she looked out on the vista spread before her.

He kept rubbing her hands, to stimulate and ease them. "Over there," he said, nodding at a mountain that loomed across the cloud-filled valley. "That's Ra-Koma. That's the Mount of Cloudy Gods. That's where we're going. With luck we can make it in another day and a half."

"But," Josie said, bewildered, staring at the soaring multicolored splendor of Ra-Koma, "to go up that…"

"To go up that, we have to go down this mountain first. Good girl. Right. You've got it." He had taken the small first-aid kit from one of his multitude of pockets and was cleaning her cuts and scrapes.

"Down," Josie mumbled, looking down into the valley, which seemed infinitely far away. "Now we have to go down?"

He nodded again. He held her hands tightly, as if willing his own strength into her. "Right, Josie, now we go down the mountain. You can do it. You're going to do it. You're strong enough to do it twice if you had to. Your hands don't hurt. Look, they're well."

He kissed one of her scraped hands. His sculptured mouth was firm and hot and moist against her skin. It was like a friendly, healing flame held against her flesh. He kissed the web of skin between her thumb and forefinger. Then he kissed her other hand, and then the first again.

"You're going to make it, Josie," he urged. He took her face between his hands. "We're going to make it together. We're going to get your Moon Flower. You're going to make it. Do you hear me?"

"I hear you, Whitewater," she said woodenly. Somehow he made her wasted strength surge back. When he stood, taking her by the hands again, she stood with him.

Together they started down the mountain.

THE TRAIL WENT DOWN and down. If Mala Lui were not so beautiful, with its rainbow of red and gray volcanic stone, its green mantle, Josie would have sworn that she was descending into hell. Mechanically, unthinkingly, she trusted Whitewater to get her to the valley. And he did.

The large and yawning cave that would shelter them resembled the famous Fern Grotto on the Hawaiian island of Kauai. By the light of the fire, Josie could see the dark glitter of foliage on the cavern walls, the shadows of the ferns that hung so uncannily from the grotto's roof. There were three springs within the cave, one, volcanically heated, that steamed in the cool evening air.

Whitewater made Josie strip and soak in the hot pool while he cooked their supper—more trout, speared from the stream that ran from the cave into the valley.

Too tired to be self-conscious, Josie took off everything except her bra and panties and slipped into the steaming pool. It felt like balm.

She leaned back and watched dazedly as Whitewater crouched over the fire. He was a man full of miracles. If there was a mountain to get up, somehow he bore her up it. If there was a mountain to descend, somehow he made it possible for her to descend. Then he parked her in a natural hot tub, speared a few trout and fixed her a meal. Truly, she thought, she should marry such a man.

Wrapped cozily in her blanket, she ate supper. Trout, coffee, biscuits—another miracle—some kind of root that Whitewater had found, which tasted vaguely like parsnips.

"Better?" he asked, as she leaned against a conveniently placed boulder, cradling her cup between her throbbing hands.

"Maybe," she said, smiling shyly at him across the camp fire. "Or maybe I died up there someplace, and this is heaven—a hot bath, a fire, a cup of coffee..."

"It can't be heaven," he observed dryly. Shadows danced with golden light across his strong features. "I'm here."

That he was there might have been the final proof she was in heaven, Josie thought, but she could not tell him that. "Thanks, Whitewater," she managed to say, looking down into her cup. "You practically carried me today. You took good care of me. I appreciate it."

One of his typical maddening silences followed. She heard the bubbling of the stream, the cry of a distant night bird. At last he answered, "It's just a job. I do it."

They weren't the words she had hoped to hear. She wasn't sure what she had hoped for. Her shoulders slumped a bit. She would have to always remember what he'd said: it was just a job. She supposed women fell in love with him all the time, and that was simply another aspect of his job, one he liked or disliked depending on the woman.

She lifted her chin. She was overcome by the strangeness of everything, that was all, and half-drunk with fatigue. She could no more actually love this man than she could sprout wings tomorrow and fly to the top of Ra-Koma. They were too different. Chance had flung them together, and when all this was over, chance would let them drift apart, and it was for the best.

She finished her coffee. He rose and poured her the last cup. "How do you know the way so precisely?" she asked. "You seem to know every nook and cranny of this mountain—this whole place."

"I've come this way before," he said, stirring the coals.

Her eyes widened in surprise. "Exactly this way?" she asked in disbelief. "Whatever for?"

"To hunt," he stated simply. He began to scrub out the frying pan with a palm frond and ashes.

"To hunt," she echoed, incredulous. "You made this hellish trek just to hunt?"

"It's what I do," he repeated stonily.

She shook her head, rejecting the truth of what he said. "I can't believe you'd come all this way just to kill something," she stated ruefully.

"I told you," he answered, "I don't particularly like the killing. I like the hunting."

"And I told you I can't understand it," she returned unhappily.

"Look," he muttered between his teeth, "maybe a woman can't understand it. Especially a woman like you. But this is what men were made by nature to do— hunt. We're an aggressive sex, and nature made us that way, too. This way, hunting, aggression is used the way it was meant to be—for survival, for being at one with nature instead of against it. I don't hunt in order to kill. I have to kill once in a while to be able to hunt."

"It makes no sense," Josie said, turning her face so that her cheek rested against the cool stone.

"It does make sense," he insisted grimly. "And you of all people ought to know that hunters have done more than any other group to conserve wildlife. Because of controlled hunting practices, there are more deer in North America than when Columbus landed."

"And the wolf is practically extinct," argued Josie.

"Be sentimental about wolves if a pack of them swarms around your door," he rasped. "Then I don't think you'll be so noble. You'll be wishing for something else—namely a good rifle."

"Whitewater," she said wearily, "didn't we have this argument in Chicago?"

"Yes," he answered, rising and kicking apart the embers of the dying fire. "We did. Go to bed, Josie."

He nodded toward the shadows, where once again he had heaped ferns and put the two ground cloths and his own blanket.

She looked up at his form, dappled with the faint light of fire glow. "What are you going to do?" she asked timorously. Climbing between the blankets with this man suddenly seemed like the most troubling thought in the world.

He gestured toward the volcanic pool. "Clean up," he said curtly. "I've got a few kinks in the muscles from lugging you around all day. And I guess I better get into shape to do it again tomorrow."

She rose, and by the dying light of the fire made her way to the bed of ferns. "I'll do better tomorrow," she said between clenched teeth. "I'll try not to be such a . . . damned burden to you."

She knelt and started to adjust the blankets.

"Yes," he answered laconically, "try that."

She turned from him, wrapping the blankets around her and lying down. She peeled off her damp underclothes and discarded them, burrowing more deeply into the blankets. His words stung like evil wasps. She had done her best today, and it hadn't been good enough. She bit her lip. Tears burned her eyes and she blinked them back. The ultimate weakness would be to let them fall.

She was still awake when he raised the blanket and lowered his body next to her tense one. Hard-muscled and warm, scented only with cleanness, he stretched out beside her.

Although she could feel the heat of him, he did not try to touch her. Her body stiffened even more, feeling the rejection in his. She bit her lip again. Again she fought back the tears. She would not cry in front of him. She would die first.

"What's wrong?" he breathed tautly, and she could feel him rising on one elbow and staring through the darkness at her.

She wanted to whip out some retort that would wound him as he had wounded her, but she could not. She had to tell him the truth. "I'm frightened," she said in a choked voice.

She sensed him there, his face close above hers. "What are you frightened of?" he asked quietly. His husky voice was edged with doubt.

"I'm afraid for Moon Flower," she said in the same strangled whisper. "I'm afraid for her baby. And for my sister."

There was a beat of silence. The sound of the rushing stream came from the front of the grotto. "We're going to get them," he told her.

The stream rolled on in the darkness, singing its secret songs. Josie looked up at him, but he was only shadow against darker shadow. She could only feel his presence.

"I'm afraid for me, too," she admitted unhappily. "I'm afraid I won't make it." A small sob escaped her, and she hated herself. She bit her fist, trying to choke back the sound of her own weakness.

"Josie, Josie," he murmured, taking her in his arms, "you're going to make it. I told you so. Trust me. I didn't mean to hurt your feelings. I spoke in anger. You've done better than most men could do. Believe me."

Desperately she wound her arms around the column of his neck. "I am," she told him with terrible earnestness. "I'm scared."

"Don't be scared," he ordered. "Hang on to me. Hang on to me as tight as you can."

Compulsively she clung to him, and his arms tightened around her, pulling her even closer to him. She felt the smooth hard spread of his chest pressing against her bare breasts and warming them with the heat of his life.

"Whitewater...?" she murmured, because his lips were so close to hers.

"I'm here," he said, his breath warm against her mouth. "And you're safe because I've got you. Understand? I've got you."

He lowered his face to hers and his warm mouth commandeered hers, a sweet piracy of touch. His hands moved over her smooth body, his long legs intertwined with hers. His lips explored her soft trembling ones, tasting them in a dozen ways and never leaving them. Josie gasped with the joyousness of his possessive kiss, and when she did, his tongue delved her mouth, and tasted her more intimately still.

His hands glided upward and covered the tender peaks of her breasts. She trembled against him, and his touch became more teasing, more demanding. He reluctantly drew his mouth from hers, then let his heated lips explore the tender hollow of her throat, the satiny skin of her collarbone, then the valley between her throbbing breasts.

The warmth of his skin beneath her hands seemed to burn her. She wound her fingers in the silky darkness of his thick damp hair. His lips retraced their tantalizing journey, lingering on her throat again, the curve of her jaw, plunging to take her mouth again and drink so deeply of it he must surely taste her soul.

His nakedness against hers was like a drug that made her yearn for more. He held her, and the darkness held them both—and secrets that her body craved to learn. Eagerly her lips sought to satisfy the questing hunger of his. His hands caressed her, moving sensously from her breasts to her thighs and back again.

"Josie," he breathed against her lips, "you feel so beautiful. I wish I could see you. But all I can do is touch and taste. But the touch and taste of you is so...beautiful."

He kissed her again, his tongue teasing hers. He wrapped one long arm about her, drawing her body as close to his as possible. His other hand traced the line of her cheekbone, her eyebrow, ran itself through the tendrils of her hair, returned to frame the curve of her jaw.

Far away, the night bird cried again. Its harsh voice seemed to warn: "No! No! Oh no, oh no, oh no!"

The cry echoed eerily in the darkness. It gave them both a second's pause, as if they each understood the urgency of that warning.

"This shouldn't happen, should it?" she asked, breaking the kiss and speaking the words against the heat of his neck. "And if it does happen, it won't mean anything to you, will it?" She felt his muscles tighten, his big body go ominously still.

"It doesn't have to mean anything, Josie," he said quietly. "All we have to do is let it be—if we want it. I thought you did."

The quiet between them was suddenly fraught with unspoken tension. He waited, in the darkness, for her to say the right thing. She was supposed to let go, to slip into the darkness entwined with his strong body, and she was supposed to say, "Yes, I want it, let it be. And it doesn't have to mean anything."

But that would be a lie. She did want her body to join with his, but she wanted it to have meaning. She wanted it to mean everything.

He drew back from her, something in his movement almost like strained ferocity. "I think you just need to be held, Josie. You don't really want to make love. Maybe you're not woman enough. But it's all right. I'm still here. And you can still hang on to me. And I'll hold you. For as long as you need holding."

His arms folded around her with an almost relentless gentleness. He laid her head against the velvety smoothness of his chest, his fingers in her hair.

"Aaron . . ." she said helplessly. How could she explain that it was love that kept her from making love, that her need of him was greater than she could make him understand?

"Call me Whitewater," he said, his voice steely. "Go to sleep, Josie. I told you, everything's all right. I've got you."

"Whitewater," she said miserably against his chest, "I'm sorry."

"Don't be," he informed her tightly. "This is just my job."

Only the insurmountable depths of her exhaustion let her fall asleep in his sheltering but dangerous arms.

CHAPTER FIVE

"Something strange is going on." Whitewater's voice had an ominous edge.

Josie blinked sleepily and raised herself on her elbow. Whitewater stood at the opening of the grotto, his large form silhouetted against the dim morning light. He was shirtless.

A small fire burned within the cavern, built on the ashes of last night's flames. Once again the odor of coffee wafted on the air and fish sizzled in the pan, but Josie was disturbed by the coiled alertness in Whitewater's manner.

She reached for her clothes and quickly tugged them on, then ran her fingers through her auburn curls and got up. She went to stand beside Whitewater and stared out at the light mist that cloaked the ferns and trees of the valley.

"I don't like it," he said, his eyes narrowing. She shivered slightly in the morning chill. What did he see? What did he sense? She didn't know, but it made her uneasy.

"What is it?" she questioned. She didn't want to look up at him. Memories of last night came tumbling back to take up painful residence among her thoughts.

"No birds are singing," he answered, a muscle twitching in one tanned cheek.

She listened. Except for the anxious rushing of the stream there was no sound at all, not even a breeze.

"It's misty," she offered.

He did not look at her, either. "It's more than that," he asserted grimly. But if he knew precisely what it was, he did not tell her, and from his bearing, the set of his jaw, she knew better than to ask.

He shook his head, pulling himself back to the business at hand. "Let's eat," he said abruptly. They both sat cross-legged by the little fire. Neither of them mentioned the night before. Neither of them, in fact, seemed to have anything to say at all.

"Perch," Josie said at last, feeling ineffectual. "You caught perch this morning. How?"

He patted one of the pockets of his field pants. "Got a fishing line and hook. No mystery," he muttered and lapsed back into silence.

"What do you keep in all those pockets, anyway?" she asked in frustration. She wished he'd put on his shirt. His broad chest distracted and disturbed her. She remembered the feel of it against her bare skin.

"Stuff," he answered with maximum vagueness. "Are you going to ask questions all morning, or are you going to get ready to go?"

She set down her cup and metal dish. She rose. He could wash the dishes, she thought uncharitably. It was his job. She turned her back on him and began to gather her things. She made her bedroll so compact that even Whitewater would have to approve, and she fastened it on her shoulders herself this time, with no help from him.

As usual he worked more quickly than she did, and he was ready to go as she struggled with the last knot. He observed her expressionlessly. "You learn fast," he said without emotion as she nodded, signaling that she was ready to go.

"Yes," she replied, looking him in the eye for the first time. "I do."

And I've learned about you, her defiant gaze told him. *I won't make the same mistake again.*

His implacable dark eyes sent a searing message of their own: *Don't play with fire, lady. It burns.*

She shrugged impatiently under the now familiar weight of the bedroll. "Let's go," she snapped. "I'm not paying you to stand around."

He put on his hat and pulled the brim down over his eyes. "Right," he said sarcastically. "Come on, Sheena of the Jungle."

They spent the morning trudging across the valley. The foilage was lusher here, the hibiscus thicker and more laden with bloom. A cloud cover hung grayly overhead, and twice a light rain fell.

Josie was grateful to note that her body seemed to be adjusting to the rigors of their journey. Her aches were fewer today, her whole body seemed unusually alive, ready for action. On the level ground she almost kept pace with Whitewater, who was maintaining his silence.

The light mist shifted about them in cloudy veils. Whitewater was right. There was an undefinable strangeness in the air. Although the sun had long been up, still no birds sang. None even appeared. The unnatural stillness was more oppressive than the gray clouds looming above them.

They forded a swift stream that came above Josie's waist. The force of the current rushed so strongly it nearly knocked her off her feet. For the first time that day, Whitewater touched her, his hand shooting out to seize her arm.

He drew her to him, holding her tightly against his side so that he took the force of the current first. With his other arm he held his rifle high.

She waded unwillingly beside him, setting her muscles to resist the smashing force of the water, unhappy that she remained standing only because his body shielded hers, his strong arm held her up. It made her dependent on his height, his power, his determination, and she didn't like it.

He released her as they reached the black-pebbled shore. The bronzed hand that had held her so securely against him dropped away. Mechanically he checked the numerous pockets of his bush vest, as if they were more important than she was.

She adjusted her sodden jeans. She shot him an ungrateful look. "Thanks," she said insincerely.

"Think nothing of it," he answered, pulling his hat brim down further over his eyes and taking the lead.

I don't think anything of it, Josie thought bitterly, following his broad back as he made a path through the bamboo. *I know it's just your job. Damn you.*

By noon they had reached the base of Ra-Koma, the Mount of Cloudy Gods, but Whitewater didn't pause. He started up. Straight up, it seemed to Josie, whose rebellion swiftly dissipated. Her heart sank at the prospect of the new steep before them.

Once more she was forced to depend on Whitewater, to feel his hands on her again and again as he helped her negotiate the sheer slopes of Ra-Koma's base.

In a scenario now all too familiar, Josie watched Whitewater forging ahead of her, somehow going up heights no normal human being would attempt. She clambered after him, but repeatedly he had to turn, regarding her dispassionately, and offer her his hand. Clasping it, she gritted her teeth and relied on his force to draw her higher up the mountain.

Sometime around one o'clock they were moving through the heavy cloud cover that clung to the lower half of the mountain. Rain and mist had made the lava slopes slippery and more difficult than ever to negotiate.

Once again, Josie forced herself to keep going by imagining Moon Flower's round, innocent black-and-white face. She prayed that Bettina was somehow keeping the panda and herself safe. Of the baby panda, she no longer dared to think or hope at all.

She had resigned herself to another afternoon of having Whitewater's hands constantly assisting her when he muttered, "It's going to get tricky here. We're going to have to thread a few needles."

He had her by the hand and was pulling her up to a dull orange shelf of lava. Panting, she found herself beside him on the narrow ledge. It was such a small outcropping that she was forced to stand only inches from him.

She looked up into his impassive face. His jaw was shadowed with slight stubble, which made his high cheekbones seem to stand out more prominently than ever. His dark eyes regarded her with a wry scientific interest. His breathing was slightly ragged.

"Thread needles?" Josie breathed, her heart suddenly slamming against her ribs. She felt dizzied and hoped it was the height, not the nearness of Whitewater that was making her blood race so.

He nodded, glancing up briefly, then returning his gaze to her. She looked up. Another ledge overhung this one, but by a geological freak, it had a hole in its center, large enough for a man to crawl through.

"We're going through *that*?" she murmured uneasily. The hole was at least three feet above her head.

"Do you see another way?" Whitewater asked sarcastically.

She glanced down. She supposed it was good the cloud cover hid exactly how high they had come. It was, she knew with sick certainty, a long fall.

"I can't reach that," she said nervously. She wished there were a way to shift on the narrow ledge so that she didn't have to stand so maddeningly close to him.

"Where there's a will there's a way," he muttered, his hands settling on her waist and gripping her tightly. Josie gasped as he pulled her even nearer to him. Then, with a groan of effort, he lifted her straight up toward the opening.

"Hey!" he ordered, "don't kick. We'll both fall off this mountain. Grab the rock. Pull yourself up."

Wildly Josie clasped the edges of the opening and tried to pull herself up. "I'm not strong enough," she panted.

He grunted and hoisted her higher still. Her head and shoulders were through the opening, but still her hold was not sure enough to allow her to pull herself up.

"My arms," she said in panic, "they're just not strong enough."

"When you get back to the mainland," groaned Whitewater, one hand moving to her hips, "work on your upper body strength, will you? I love your anatomy, but your biceps, at present, leave a lot to be desired."

Josie felt his hand gripping her bottom unceremoniously. Her mind flashed a terrifying image: the two of them losing their balance and plunging down the mountainside.

"Whitewater," she protested weakly, "I don't think this is a good idea."

"Then don't go around losing your pandas," he answered between his teeth. He somehow had both hands under her hips now, and seemed to be lifting her up primarily by the force of determination.

Josie tried to ignore the intimate and slightly undignified contact he was making with her body. He had raised her high enough that she could pull herself the rest of the way through the opening. With a gasp she did so, like a swimmer clambering heavily out of a pool.

She lay on the ledge, her heart hammering and her hips tingling. "Here," Whitewater ordered, and handed up his rifle. She took it, and then rolled wearily to the side. This ledge, at least, was wider than the first.

She saw Whitewater's hands at the edge of the hole. She heard another determined groan. Fearfully she watched as he drew himself up. His teeth were gritted with the effort as he exerted enough strength to get his head and shoulders through the opening. With a pained grimace, he exerted a last spurt of force and wrestled his way up to lie beside her.

He rolled onto his back, stared into the grayness of the cloud a moment. "We're having some fun now, eh?" he asked ironically, then took a deep breath.

Josie stared at his profile as he caught his breath. "I never," she said, still panting with exertion and fright, "want to do anything like that again."

"Too bad," he answered raggedly. "Look up."

She looked up and swallowed hard. Another ledge, narrower than this, another hole, slightly smaller. "Another one?" she asked in pained disbelief.

"Two more," he said with unpleasant matter-of-factness. "And what are you complaining about? I have to do all the work."

Josie sat up and glared down at him. His eyes were closed momentarily, his long lashes black against his coppery skin. "It's not exactly a pleasure for me having your hands all over my—all over me," she informed him haughtily.

He opened one eye, gave her a dubious look, then shut it again. "You have very firm buttocks," he said. "My congratulations. That makes my part of the job more pleasant, though not any easier."

He sighed and got up, drawing her to her feet beside him. "I don't like this—" she began, but he cut her off.

"No other choice," he said curtly. He lifted her up, and this time immediately got hold around her hips and kept pushing her upward.

"Watch those hands, Whitewater!" Josie cried irately, as their contact became even more personal. Her embarrassment almost overcame her dread as she struggled awkwardly for a handhold.

"Honey," he said from beneath her, his voice pained, "get used to it. By the time I get you up this mountain, I'm going to have to touch you just about everywhere you can be touched. It's nothing personal."

"I know," Josie tossed back, now managing to crawl to safety on the second ledge. "It's just your job."

She watched, half fearful, half respectful as he managed to hoist himself through the second opening. Again he lay for a moment beside her, regaining his breath. "What a job," he said laconically. "I could be off somewhere fighting a nice shark or something. I hope you appreciate this."

Josie cast him a fiery blue-green glance. The lower half of her body burned from his intimate touching and grasping. "More than you know," she said ironically.

He sighed harshly and stood again. "Come on," he said. "One more time. We're starting to get good at this."

He reached down and pulled her to her feet. Again he put his hands around her waist. For a moment he stared down into her eyes. A smile played at the corner of his mouth, disappeared, then came back. "I wish somebody cared as much about me as you care about that panda," he muttered.

Josie looked back at him, confusion filling her heart. "Maybe if you were more of a gentleman, somebody would," she returned, fighting back her feelings for him.

"No chance of that," he said with stoic cheer and lifted her up. In a few seconds, his hands were clasping her in places no gentleman would clasp.

"Watch it, Whitewater," she warned again, trying to get a purchase on the opening.

"I am watching it," he said insolently. "And it's cute as the dickens."

AFTER THEY HAD THREADED the third needle eye, the slope of the mountain gentled mercifully. Still Whitewater didn't stop, although Josie felt almost faint with hunger. Fatigue settled on her like a familiar garment by the middle of the afternoon. It weighed so heavily that she almost forgot her discomfiture at the way Whitewater had touched her when they climbed the three ledges.

The experience seemed to have put him in better humor, although he still looked around from time to time with an air of unrest. They were past the cloud cover now, hiking up the emerald-cloaked slope of the middle of Ra-Koma. The sun shone down hotly, but now the birds sang as normal and the breeze moved as usual.

Whitewater had taken off his shirt and tied it by the arms around his waist. His arms and chest were naked under his open bush vest, and he carried the rifle casually across both shoulders, like a soldier who is an old hand at such things. He felt good enough, apparently, to whistle, which he did very badly. Unfortunately he seemed to know only one tune, which was "Waltzing Matilda."

Josie trudged beside him in the hot sunshine. "Can't you enlarge your repertoire?" she asked at last, irritably.

"Nope," he said cheerfully and resumed his whistling.

"What is it you like so much about that song?" she demanded.

"The words," he answered.

"Then why are you whistling?" she grumbled. "You can't whistle words."

"Doesn't matter," he replied. "I think them." He continued his off-key whistle.

"I thought Indians were supposed to be quiet and serious and dignified," she muttered. And not so dratted mercurial, she added mentally.

"Vicious rumors," he replied and smiled at her wickedly. "Stereotypes. Like redheads are supposed to be sexy. A man could be in trouble if he believed that."

I hate you, Whitewater, she thought darkly. *I really hate you.*

He acted as if he knew, and it made him more obnoxiously cheerful than before.

BY SIX O'CLOCK the forest had thinned again, and the sun cast long soft shadows. Whitewater deigned to look down at Josie. He nodded upward. "We're going over that next ridge," he informed her, "and then we're stopping for the night."

"Stopping?" Josie asked, relieved. She had begun to believe, dully, that Whitewater was going to go on forever.

"Stopping," he repeated. "We've covered more ground than I'd hoped. We can make the plantation tomorrow morning. Besides, we could use a swim and a rest."

"A swim?" she asked, brightening slightly.

"Of course," he said with his white grin. "This is the South Pacific, remember? As close to paradise as a mortal is likely to get. Swimming pools all over the place—if you know where to look."

Paradise, she thought, struggling to keep up with him. If this was paradise, she'd had little time to enjoy it. Paradise was spoiled by a serpent named Lucas, who lurked at the mountaintop. Or by one named Whitewater, who was more subtle and wily and unpredictable than any beast of the field.

Or by one named desire that lay dangerous and secret, coiled in her own heart.

"OH, TAKE OFF your clothes," Whitewater said in disgust. He had already flung off his bush vest and sat at the pool's ferny edge, taking off his heavy boots. "I've already felt most of you today. What difference does it make if I see you? Besides, we've slept together naked. Grow up, Josie."

"That's different," she insisted stubbornly, although the blue depths of the pool looked deliciously inviting. "And don't you dare take off all your clothes, either."

"Why?" He smirked. His dark forelock had fallen over his brow and he looked out from beneath it wickedly. "Afraid things will get out of hand again? It's all right. I can resist temptation for two. I'll save you from yourself."

She finished the snack of dried fruit she was eating. She stood up and spanked her hands clean. "You're incorrigible," she accused. "And I want you to know I'm not sleeping with you tonight. I'd rather freeze."

"Fine," he answered, standing himself. "Freeze. You moan and groan all night long anyway. About your sister. And your everlasting panda."

He unzipped his field pants and stepped out of them. Josie looked away but couldn't help seeing him. His body was magnificent. He wore only the briefest of khaki briefs, which, mercifully, he kept on. But the width of his shoulders, the hard bronze of his chest, the leanness of his stomach and the incredibly muscled length of his thighs made her suck in a breath so sharply that her chest hurt.

He stood, poised briefly, on the stone overhang, then dived cleanly into the pool. He rose to the surface, shaking water from his dark hair. "It feels great," he taunted. "Come on in. Wear your underwear. Excuse me, your lingerie."

"Oh, all right," Josie agreed grumpily. Whitewater grinned and dived again. She kicked off her high boots and stripped off her socks. She shed her teal-blue knit shirt and her jeans. She stood for a moment on the overhang, wondering just how incongruous her lacy aqua bra and panties looked in the middle of the forest of Ra-Koma. Then she made a perfect swan dive into the sapphire depths of the pool.

She arose gasping at the cool hospitality of the water. She shook droplets from her hair. Whitewater surfaced beside her. "Ah," he said. "Just how much have you taken off?" Beneath the water, he ran his hands familiarly from her hips to beneath her arms, grazing the lace cups of the bra that held her swelling breasts.

"Go away," she ordered, swimming backward, "or I'll drown you."

"You won't drown me," he teased, pursuing her with long clean strokes. "Who'd catch your supper? And who'd cook it? Who'd build the fire?"

"Who cares?" she asked saucily, swimming away from him. "I'd get your blanket, and not have to put up with you."

"For such ingratitude, I'll drown you instead," he threatened, putting on a burst of speed. He dived suddenly, and Josie felt herself pulled down by her ankles. Quickly she took a large breath of air and surrendered to the deep.

Effortlessly Whitewater kept her beneath the blue water, while his hands climbed higher up her legs. Then he seized her completely and rose with her to the surface, holding her in his arms and treading water.

"Abandon hope," he ordered. "You've been captured by the Sioux. Prepare for a fate worse than death."

She laughed, and allowed herself the dangerous luxury of putting her arms around his neck to maintain her balance.

"I think," he muttered as he gained a foothold and stood chest deep in the water, still holding her tightly, "that after a day like today, though, we should smoke the peace pipe. Agreed?"

She looked into his brown-black eyes, his lashes starred with water. "I guess we should," she breathed reluctantly.

"We've had ourselves a day, eh, Josie?" he asked companionably. "And now we're almost there. Someday this will make a tale to tell, as the old men used to say."

"A tale to tell?" she asked, resisting the impulse to lay her hand on his smoothly muscled chest.

"That's what the old braves used to say when taking crazy chances: *hoka hey!* Let's make a tale to tell. Do something worth remembering."

"I'm not sure today will be worth remembering," she replied doubtfully, suddenly uneasy at his nearness. "I never thought we'd get this far. It might be best forgotten."

"No," he answered, the joking suddenly gone from his voice. "It's worth remembering. The needles' eyes had me worried. But we made it. I think it's worth congratulating ourselves for."

He looked down at her so intently that Josie's heart felt shaken. She wondered if he could see it beating beneath the wet lace of her bra. She was powerless to let her gaze leave his. Slowly his eyes dropped to the vulnerable softness of her mouth.

"Congratulations," she said so low that it was almost a whisper. But the word was already superfluous, too late, for he was bending his face to kiss her, and she was lifting her own to accept it.

His mouth was at first cool against hers, then warm, then hot, as the kiss deepened and his lips bore down on hers more intently. Her heart pounded so hard that her whole body trembled. She could not draw her mouth away from his, but instead tremulously raised her face to give her lips to his more completely.

He kissed her as if it were his right to do so, and his alone, and he savored the power he possessed. His hand moved to caress the damp tendrils of her hair, then trace the delicate inner curve of her ear.

She trembled even more violently against him. Helpless to resist, she let her lips part so that his tongue could enter, gently ravishing hers.

His fingers moved to frame her chin and lift her face higher yet, so that he drank her kisses even more deeply, as a man might drink magic wine. Josie felt herself becoming lost in the strength and demand of his embrace. He stroked his knuckles against the cool smoothness of her cheek, ran his fingers once more through the fiery wealth of her hair.

Then his lips moved from hers, leaving her breathing fast and shallow with desire. He rained kisses on her temple, her feathery eyebrow, her closed eyelids, her cheek, the wildly beating pulse at the base of her jaw.

She answered by kissing his naked shoulder, which tasted like sunshine and the diamond spray of the water. His tongue traced a moistly fiery line down the tender cord of her throat, then nibbled erotically at the smooth curve where neck joined shoulder. His lips explored her shoulder slowly, and with a soft, tormenting thoroughness.

Then he bent her head more firmly against the breadth of his own shoulder, lifted her hair, and kissed her neck, his tongue setting shivering flames aglow in her sensitive nape.

Her arms remained wound around his neck, as if she would slip away into the outer reaches of space if she let go of the vital force of him. But his hands wandered now to her body, caressing first her bare waist with maddening languor, then the ripe curves of her lace-clad hips, the long sweep of her smooth outer thigh, the softness and secrecy of her inner thigh, the flatness of her stomach.

His lips returned to hers, as a conquering monarch returns to claim his appointed treasure. Gladly she gave herself to his capture. She barely noticed when the damp lace of her bra somehow slipped away from her full, tingling breasts. His hands covered their lovely naked pink tips, making them swell like burgeoning buds beneath his touch. Her rosy nipples ached for more of him, and when he lowered his mouth to take first one and then the other between his lips, she shuddered again, so hard this time, he clasped her even closer, as if to protect her from the power of her own desire.

Lingeringly, slowly, with infinite patience and savoring, he tasted and teased first one erect tip, then the other. Then he took them gently in his hands as he pressed his face between her breasts to trail his tongue through the heated valley.

He paused, sighing harshly, long enough to carry her to shallower water. Gently he stood her so that the water lapped at her thighs. Again he lowered his head to her breast and teased first one, then the other, to tingling ecstasy.

He dropped to his knees, letting his kisses trail down her flat stomach. His hands moved to cover her hips, drawing her body even nearer to his kneeling one. Gently he began to lower the clinging lace panties.

"No!" Josie shuddered, stepping back. "Aaron, no, please. You promised."

He ignored her protest, pulling her near again, and placed a heated kiss on the edge of the wet lace. Josie's knees trembled. She wanted nothing more than to sink to her own knees and let him take her lips again, to hold her so tightly that her straining breasts might be satisfied by the crushing pressure of his chest.

But this was insanity. She had spent all day telling herself so. She had sworn last night that she would never let this man touch her in this way again. Now she had not only allowed it, she wanted it so much she ached.

In one fluid motion, he stood again, towering over her. His eyes were black as onyx. His hands slid up from her hips to her rib cage, his thumbs beneath her breasts, his fingers framing them with sure gentleness.

"Don't tell me you don't want me," he challenged, his voice ominously low. "I know we want each other. I knew it clear back in Chicago."

She stared up at him helplessly. Her hands rested ineffectually on the rippling muscles of his biceps, and her skin looked as pale as petals next to his sun-bronzed flesh. "You promised," she repeated, her voice quivering. The complexity of her emotions overwhelmed her. She wanted him. She feared wanting him. She feared herself.

"Sometimes promises should be broken," he said huskily. "There are things stronger than promises. That's why I don't like making them. I'd rather be free. Free to make love to you."

Her gaze wavered. She stared again at her pale, city-girl's hands against his hard, tanned skin. "And free to go your own way afterward," she murmured, ashamed for caring.

Once again his hand was beneath her chin, turning her face up to his. "We'll both be free to go our ways,

Josie," he said softly. "These few days we have are something we'll never have again. Something we'd be foolish to waste. You don't want promises from me. You've told me too many times how different we are. And you're right. But sometimes, like now, differences don't matter. Let's take what life has to offer us to-day—and not ask questions about tomorrow. Or make promises about it."

Still she could not meet his eyes. He was being honest, she knew. How odd, she thought bitterly, nibbling at her lower lip. If only he were cold-blooded enough to tell her a pretty lie or two. Even if she knew they were lies, how much easier it would be to give herself to him as she wanted.

She took her hands from his arms. She crossed her arms covering her breasts. She raised her eyes to him again. "Unfortunately, Whitewater," she said, her voice strained, "tomorrow usually has a way of rolling around. Let's disregard this incident. And *I'll* be the one who makes sure it doesn't happen again. In my sunset years I don't want to look back and have to remember I couldn't resist some macho opportunist—just because the breeze was balmy, the water was blue, and I was tired out of my mind."

His face went suddenly hard. He didn't try to restrain her when she pulled away from him. She managed to walk with remarkable natural dignity up the bank of the pool and to the overhang. She shrugged back into her shirt, pulled on her jeans.

She looked down into the pool. He was swimming again, with almost vicious concentration. He looked up at her and their eyes locked for an interminable moment, private fires leaping between them.

He smiled, crooking one dark brow sardonically. "Fine," he said, looking her up and down with his old mocking, measuring look. "Just remember—it's your loss."

His arrogance stung. She glared down at him. "The only loss I regret is Moon Flower. Keep your hands off me and your mind on her." She turned her back on him and walked away again.

Half an hour later, when he was dressed again, he knelt to build one of his economical fires. He had caught a brace of small catfish. Josie sat on a stone, trying to ignore him while he fanned the twigs into life.

He looked at her only once. "Hey!" he said abruptly. She turned slightly, giving him a cool glance.

"This is yours," he said with a sneer. He reached into a pocket and pulled out a sodden little turquoise ball. He tossed it so that it landed at her booted feet. "You seemed to have lost track of it."

It was her bra. She picked it up and thrust it angrily into her own pocket. They ate in silence. They bedded down separately.

Josie fell asleep in spite of the chill of the mountain night and her own tumultuous emotions. She did not know when, in the middle of the night, Whitewater came to her side, silent as a shadow, and wrapped his own blanket around her tightly curled form.

He sat up for a long time, listening to the cries of the night creatures. Then he lay down uncovered in the cold. He thought of his grandfather. *"Lela Oosni."* He muttered the Sioux words between his teeth: *very cold.* But whether he was talking about the night or the woman, he wasn't sure. Perhaps he was even speaking of his own heart, which he had long ago taught to bear the cold, and to bear it alone. He didn't need this stubborn woman, he told himself, staring into the darkness. He only wanted her, for just a little while, and he could not even say why.

CHAPTER SIX

THE FIRST LIGHT of dawn barely filtered down through the still leaves. Whitewater's hands gripped Josie's arms, drawing her up to his kneeling figure. His face was close to hers. "Wake up," he demanded, his voice husky in her ear. "Hurry. We've got trouble."

Chilled and groggy, Josie welcomed the warmth of his big body. She shut her eyes more tightly and tried to lay her head against the comforting breadth of his chest. But he made her sit erect. He shook her slightly.

She blinked at him sleepily. The morning air felt cold on her bare shoulders, and she pulled the blankets more tightly around her. *Blankets?* she thought in confusion. How did she get two blankets? Had he given her his? Her first impulse was to curl happily into Whitewater's arms, but her more rational mind recoiled from him. She had told him to keep his hands off her.

"Don't touch me," she muttered, wriggling free from his grasp. "What do you want? Is breakfast ready?"

"Who wants to touch you?" he snapped back, releasing her without protest. He stood up. "Get dressed. You can eat on the trail. I told you, we've got trouble."

She ran her fingers through her tousled auburn curls. She looked up at him dubiously. "What kind of trouble?"

He nodded to the east. "Kana-Puma," he said, staring down at her. "The volcano."

Her blue-green eyes widened, suddenly wary and alert. Her lips parted in an unspoken question.

His only show of emotion was a bitter curl at the corner of his mouth. "I think it's going to go. Come on. Let's get to the top of that mountain."

He turned his back so that she could scramble from the blankets and struggle into clean clothes. "How do you know?" she asked, her voice trembling as she tried to button her green knit shirt. She stepped into her jeans, then sat on a stone, anxiously pulling on her socks and long boots.

He turned back, as if he could sense that she was no longer naked. He began to pack their things quickly. "I don't know how," he replied simply. "I just know. There's something in the air. It was here yesterday, but it went away. I thought it was my imagination. Now it's back. Stronger than before. Listen."

She stood, her ears straining. Gradually she realized what he meant. There was nothing to listen *to*. The world seemed unnaturally silent, as if holding its breath, hoping some disaster would pass. The mountain, the foliage, the air itself seemed to wait.

The silence frightened her. Dawn was still shadowy, without brightness. She went to the pool and splashed water on her face, brushed her teeth, ran a brush through her hair. How odd, she thought, pausing long enough to put on a touch of lipstick. She had a compulsion to look her best, even in the face of an erupting volcano. Her mother would be proud.

Whitewater already had his bedroll strapped on. She didn't object when he helped her fasten hers. He gave

ARE THESE
THE KEYS TO YOUR NEW
CADILLAC COUPE DE VILLE

INSTRUCTIONS:

With a coin, scratch off the silver on your lucky keys to reveal your secret registration numbers. If they match, return this entry form—you instantly and automatically qualify to win a brand new Cadillac Coupe de Ville!

YOUR UNIQUE SWEEPSTAKES ENTRY NO.

№ -1G541954

☐ **YES,** please enter me in the Sweepstakes and tell me if I've won the $1,000,000.00 Grand Prize, or any other prize. Also send me my four *free* Harlequin Romances plus a *free* mystery gift as explained on the opposite page!

118 CIH FAVR

NAME	(PLEASE PRINT)
ADDRESS	APT.
CITY	STATE ZIP

☐ No, don't send me my free books or the free mystery gift, but do enter me in the Sweepstakes.

eturn this card **TODAY** to qualify for
ne $1,000,000.00 Grand Prize **PLUS** a
Cadillac Coupe de Ville **AND** over
5000 other cash prizes!

missing, write to: Harlequin Reader Service® 901 Fuhrmann Blvd P.O. Box 1867 Buffalo NY 14269-1867

her a drink of water from the canteen, some jerky and dried fruit.

"You're sure it's Kana-Puma?" she asked, studying his somber features. "It's really the volcano?"

He nodded, pulling his hat brim down grimly. "I know what it feels like when a storm's coming," he answered. "This is different. The wildlife knows. You can't hear so much as an insect. Come on. Let's get your sister and your panda and get the hell out of here."

He set off, shouldering his way through the brush and up the mountainside. Josie followed as swiftly as she could. She nibbled at her meager breakfast without enthusiasm. She had no appetite.

"Whitewater?" she said to his back, her voice taut. "Are we in danger? What's going to happen?"

"I don't know," he answered shortly, plunging on. "Kana-Puma's a long way to the east. I'm not worried about lava—unless this whole island decides to blow. I'm worried about the volcanic cloud, and the steam. The wind's against us."

Josie hurried after him. The stillness of the morning forest made her every movement sound desperately loud and clumsy, although ahead of her Whitewater moved almost soundlessly. She tried to still her hammering heart, force her movements to mimic the silence of his.

She racked her memory about volcanoes. She remembered, vaguely, stories of great clouds that obscured the sky for days, of dangerous steam and poisonous gases. By the time they reached the top of Ra-Koma, they should be well above the peak of the volcano.

But steams, gases, clouds, Josie reasoned worriedly, rose in the air. Even if the worst was a sky full of dust, they could be trapped. No plane could take off if the visibility was bad. And if they could not escape, they must remain for the worst that Kana-Puma could curse them. What had Horace Coelho said? That humans shouldn't trespass on the Mount of Cloudy Gods. For a moment, Josie wondered superstitiously if the island was angry.

The climb grew steeper. Wordlessly, Whitewater reached his hand back to Josie and hauled her up the steeper spots. Sometimes his dark eyes met her worried azure ones, but neither of them spoke. It was as if time was too important to waste on speaking.

The day barely brightened; the sky stayed ominously dark. After almost three hours of moving relentlessly upward, Whitewater stopped on a small plateau where a minute stream gurgled. He flung himself down beside it and told Josie to do the same. They would rest a few moments, gathering strength for the assault on the peak of Ra-Koma.

He refilled the canteen and gave Josie two protein bars, which he insisted she eat. The silence, unbroken except for the rippling of the stream, brooded about them. Still not hungry, Josie managed to eat the two bars, although they tasted like sawdust. She would have rebelled, but for Whitewater's watching eyes.

He himself ate nothing. She supposed, fretfully, he had given her his share of the scanty food. Questions that had tormented her all morning long came tumbling out nervously.

"What's the worst thing that can happen to us if Kana-Puma blows?" she asked, watching him refill the canteen.

"The worst?" He shrugged. "I go to the Happy Hunting Ground and you go to the Hereafter of your choice. But I'm not fool enough to worry about the worst. I'm worried about the most probable."

She watched him screw the top back on the canteen. "That the clouds trap us? That we can't take off?"

He nodded curtly.

Josie gave a long sigh, which turned into a shudder of frustration. "I mean," she said, her teeth clenched, "suppose we make it to the top before anything happens. Suppose we find Lucas—and we save Bettina and Moon Flower. And that you're right, there's a plane there, all fueled up and waiting to go. Do you even know how to fly one? You never told me."

He gave another of his maddening broad-shouldered shrugs. "You never asked. Yeah, I can fly. Kind of."

"Kind of?" Josie demanded, her taut nerves snapping. "What kind of answer is that? Kind of?"

He leaned back against the mossy rock, regarding her with amusement. "I used to have a licence. I haven't flown for a couple of years. I can handle it. Trust me."

Josie gazed at him, so stolid beside her. She shook her head, then buried her face in her hands. "I *have* trusted you," she muttered, "and look where it's got me. On some forbidden mountain with a volcano about to blow its top. And I don't even know if my sister and Moon Flower are up there."

"They're up there," he answered.

"And how are we supposed to get them if they are?" she asked pettishly, her face still in her hands. "Just walk up to Lucas and say, 'Excuse me, there seems to be a mistake. You have a woman we want, and our panda. We'll just take them and be on our way...' He's dangerous, you know."

There was a familiar beat of silence between them. "I can be dangerous myself," Whitewater said evenly.

She dropped her hands and stared at him in angry anxiety. "Outside of a bedroll?" she asked acidly.

He kept his face nearly expressionless. The high cheekbones, the unreadable black eyes, made him look dangerous. She regretted her words. But one corner of his well-shaped mouth crooked. "You're amazing," he muttered. "This island might blow right off the map. And when it goes, you'll still be obsessing about your damned virtue. Even lava won't warm you up. Not you."

She looked away from his mocking face, but she still burned with anger. "Just because I can resist you doesn't mean I'm terminally cold," she argued. "It simply means I've got standards. And my 'virtue' isn't the issue here. Lucas is. What are you going to do with him when you find him—*if* you find him?"

"How do I know until it happens?" he retorted easily. "I have to see what the setup is. I can't make plans until then. Then he's just like any other prey. I figure out how to take him when I see him."

Her face swiveled to look at him again. He still wore the same resolutely sardonic smile. "Aaron," she said timidly, her eyes widening slight, "you're not going to shoot him, are you?"

The smile flickered, went away, came back to taunt her. "Don't," he said softly, "call me Aaron. You don't know me well enough."

She continued to stare at him, horrified. "You won't, will you?" she asked, wondering if she did indeed know him, even slightly. "You won't hurt Lucas, will you? I can't condone violence, Whitewater."

"Can't you, Josie?" he asked, one brow rising in wry disbelief. He looked at her as one might look at an impossibly naive child. "Then what are you going to do when violence comes your way? Let it take you? And everything you love?''

She drew her gaze away and stared into the silent shadows of the forest. ''I can't allow you to hurt him,'' she stated, her voice quivering with intensity.

She felt his fingers lightly take her chin and turn her face back toward his. She looked up at him, apprehension in her eyes. ''When we get there,'' he told her, his smile gone now, ''we may have time to work out a plan, and we may not. Either way, you're going to have to do as I say, no questions asked. I'll try not to hurt Lucas unless I have to—all right? Trust me. Just trust me, Josie, it won't be much longer now.''

She tried to look away from his dark gaze and found herself staring at the handsome line of his mouth. Trust him. It kept coming back to that, and would, until Bettina and Moon Flower were both found and saved. Her breath was shallow, almost painful. The merest touch of his fingers had sent her heart galloping off again. ''I guess I don't have any choice,'' she answered.

''Good girl,'' he said, his smile returning. But it was almost kindly this time. She stayed still, almost hypnotized as he lowered his face and kissed her.

It was a long kiss, oddly gentle, as if he were saying goodbye. Yet it felt so right that Josie made no move to object. The world was silent except for the rushing of the stream and the beating of her heart. For a lingering moment, the only touch in the world was Whitewater's, sure and warm against her lips. The only light that existed was that golden fire he lit in her blood.

At last he broke the kiss, and his thumb lightly caressed the line of her jaw. ''Let's go get us a panda,'' he said, "before this place blows like a cheap fire-cracker."

"Why did you do that?" she asked softly, searching his face for an answer. "Why did you kiss me?"

He stood and gave her a hand up. His fingers released hers quickly, as if the contact between their hands were all business, no pleasure. "I don't know," he answered, shouldering his bedroll. "Maybe because it might be my last chance."

Last chance, Josie thought fatefully, following him upward again. For so long the steeps and slopes of the mountains had seemed the enemy. She realized, slightly sick, that the real enemy could be awaiting when they gained the top of Ra-Koma. The real villain was Lucas, and Lucas might be deadly. Whitewater was putting himself into great jeopardy for her—and for Bettina and Moon Flower.

She kept climbing. And in spite of her swarming worries about what lay in wait, she hoped Whitewater was wrong about at least one thing: there would, somehow, be another chance for the two of them.

THEY GAINED the top of Ra-Koma shortly before eleven in the morning. The sun was high in the sky, but pale and faint, as if it did not want to look down upon events below. The forest maintained its uneasy silence.

Whitewater signaled for her to be as quiet as possible. He took out his rifle and loaded it. Josie's mouth went dry as she watched him. His every movement was frighteningly precise.

He crept through the bamboo and pines so noiselessly it seemed the laws of sound had been temporarily suspended. Her every sense sharpened, she followed, surprised at how silent her own alertness made her.

He heard something and stopped. She listened, hearing nothing. His ears were keener than hers—she had learned that long ago. But twenty-five yards later he stopped once more, turning to her, his expression telling her clearly: listen carefully.

She heard it then, faint but unmistakable. The strange growling yip and rumbling bark that was made by only one animal on earth: the panda. Moon Flower! With a surge of joy, Josie thought, *She's alive! She's here!*

For a moment Whitewater watched the happiness lighting her face. He smiled slightly himself, then started moving again.

Josie followed him giddily. She couldn't believe the luck, the sheer miracle of it. Moon Flower was on the mountaintop, exactly as Whitewater had guessed. Her heartbeats skipped, her thoughts seemed to float happily, like shining bubbles.

Whitewater inched up a small rise, taking cover behind a stand of dark pines. Josie crept up beside him. She could hear the unmistakable intermittent cries of Moon Flower clearly now. The grunts and shrills of the panda sounded more beautiful than any music.

Standing on tiptoe, she stared between the branches, following Whitewater's gaze. The forest had taken over the plantation's abandoned buildings. They were at the edge of a ragged clearing, perhaps fifty yards from the rear of the main building. The overgrown great house was caved in, only its charred walls standing, victim of a fire, accidental or deliberate.

Between the two observers and the blackened mansion was a series of smaller buildings. In a pen to the east, just beyond the buildings, paced a chubby, round-headed animal, its black-and-white coloring dramatic against the green of the forest.

Moon Flower, as beautiful as ever, lumbered back and forth in her makeshift prison. She chewed meditatively at a stalk of cut bamboo, but did not eat it. She stared sadly through her bars with her masked eyes. She swatted at a flower that hung over her head, suspended from a vine. Then she paced again, seeming lost in her own melancholy thoughts.

Josie didn't mind when Whitewater's arm slid around her and squeezed her hard. She grinned up at him and he smiled back. He nodded to the west.

Josie followed his gaze and her smile widened. At the western edge of the clearing was a small cracked landing strip, and at its end stood a green-and-yellow twin-engine plane. The old hangar, like the main house, had caved in long ago and was covered with vines. But the plane was hidden, by a crude shelter of branches and fronds, from anyone who might fly over. Whitewater squeezed her again. Unthinkingly, almost drunk with happiness, she let her arm slide around his waist and hugged him back.

When she touched him that way, it was like the completion of an electrical circuit. A crackling energy flowed between her body and his, shocking her back to a sober reality. Quickly she drew her arm away. She looked up at him, the question clear upon her face. "What now?"

He released her as quickly as she had him. But he bent, tilting his face so that his hat brim did not graze hers. His lips brushed against her ear. "We have to see how many people are here. And find out if they're armed."

Josie nodded, then gulped slightly. Anxiously she scanned the scene before them. One of the outbuildings, perhaps once a gardener's residence or guest house, did not have the same air of desertion as the other buildings. A newly worn path led from its door and branched off in several directions: toward the panda pen, the airstrip and another smaller hut that might be used for storage.

The windows of the dilapidated little house were broken, but pushed up into an open position nonetheless. No smoke issued from its chimney, and Josie could see no movement within. Except, she thought, her gaze riveted by something moving in the grass, and something else twinkling in the weeds, someone had recently dropped a candy wrapper and tossed away a soft-drink can. And someone had thrown a filthy quilt behind the house. It lay in a multicolored heap. Beside it was a recently discarded chair that had not yet seen much of the island's wind or rain.

How like you, Lucas, she thought ironically. *You're going to save the world, but within a week you've started to trash your own environment.* The panda pen, she noted with some concern, needed cleaning. And Moon Flower's pacing and cries were somehow strange, haunting...

"Shh," Whitewater warned in her ear, as simultaneously, the door of the little house swung open. Josie stiffened, dragging her attention away from the panda. Lucas came swaggering out of the door. His shoulder-length brown hair needed washing, as did his black T-shirt and jeans. He wore, as usual, his black headband.

Behind him came another young man, whom Josie had never seen before. He was small and wiry, built along the same lean tense lines as Lucas. His dark hair was cropped closely to his head, and he wore faded denims and a checkered shirt. He looked nervous and unhappy.

A third young man followed, and he was the one that made Josie blink in fear. He was huge. He was at least as tall as Whitewater, and his body was far heavier, if flabby. Like Lucas, he swaggered, but his movements were ponderous and slow, like those of an overweight grizzly. His eyes seemed buried in the fat of his face, and his head was shaved.

All three men wore shoulder holsters. Josie swallowed hard again.

She looked nervously back at Moon Flower, who was making strange movements, almost as if some invisible partner led her in a slow, four-footed waltz. She wasn't acting normally. Perhaps the morning's strangeness, which had affected the island's other animals, was making her uneasy. Let it be that, Josie thought, pleading silently, and not—

Her attention snapped back to the door of the little house. Bettina stood there, looking after the three men. "Don't leave me, Lucas," she cried, her hands gripping the doorframe.

Lucas, heading toward the hidden plane, stopped and pivoted. "I'm not leaving you," he said in his wheedling, affected voice. "Ollie's staying with you. But I'm going to check things out in the village. Something funny's going on. I want to know what. Can't get any radio reception in this damned place."

Bettina left the doorway, running to him. Lucas gripped her elbows tightly and held her at arm's length. "Lucas," she begged, trying to move closer to him, "please don't leave me here. Everything feels . . . so strange. Even the panda's acting strange. What if she—"

Lucas tossed his long hair and rolled his pale eyes. "Take her, Ollie," he said impatiently. Josie's muscles tightened in rebellion as she saw the huge man with the shaved head step up and put his hands on Bettina's shoulders. Effortlessly he drew her away from Lucas. He backed up with her, until they both stood before a grove of stunted palms, only twenty or so yards from where Josie and Whitewater watched.

"Damn," Whitewater said softly between his teeth. "I don't like any one of them having her too close. She can be used—as a shield or a hostage."

Lucas pretended to brush dust from his black shirt. He straightened his shoulder holster. "Can you keep from panicking for once, Bettina?" he asked nastily. "Just once? I'd have never brought you along if I knew you were so undependable. I'd have taken the panda and left you sitting in Chicago. You're a weakling. How do you expect to change the world if you can't even control your own emotions?"

"Lucas..." Bettina begged, struggling to escape from Ollie's grasp. A smile crossed Ollie's flaccid features as he jerked the girl roughly back into place.

Josie felt her jaw setting hard as she watched Bettina's helplessness. Her sister looked terrible: too thin, too pale, too harried. She had lines under her eyes, and next to the massive Ollie, she looked as powerless as a child.

"Lucas," Bettina cried again, desperation in her voice, "let's all get off this island. I have the feeling something terrible is going to happen. Let's all go now. Let's give up all this craziness. If we surrender—"

Lucas nodded an order, and Ollie tightened his fat hands on Bettina so hard that the girl gasped. "If something terrible is going to happen," Lucas taunted, "then I'll be back—for the panda, but not for you, if you don't behave. Believe me, Bettina, I'd leave you here and never think twice about it. So settle down and do what I say. In the meantime, nobody's going anywhere until I put in some extra fuel. The auxiliary tanks are empty. And the regular tank is only part full."

Bettina stopped struggling against Ollie's mammoth hands. "Why didn't you get extra fuel the last time you went?" she asked, more out of fear than rebellion. "Why take the chance of being caught, or stranded here?"

Lucas laughed unpleasantly. "So somebody like you doesn't try to take off and leave *me* stranded here. Besides, I can't afford to raise suspicions by letting them know I've got auxiliary tanks—unless there's a genuine emergency. I'm not like you, Bettina. I don't panic. So pipe down. I mean it. If anything's wrong, I'll leave you here. Come on, Willis."

Lucas started toward the plane once more. The lean man named Willis shot Bettina an unhappy look, as if he would have liked to help her but couldn't. Then he plodded off after Lucas.

"They can't get away," Whitewater whispered harshly in her ear. "We need that plane."

Josie looked up at him questioningly. Lucas and Willis were moving farther from Bettina and Ollie with each step. She saw the problem immediately: how to render all three men harmless. Whitewater's rifle would have to keep three men covered at once. No easy task as spread out as they were becoming, and with Bettina vulnerable.

"How much tranquilizer did you bring for the panda?" Whitewater asked tersely.

"Immobilizing agent? Enough. Plenty. Extra. Enough for an elephant," she answered in confusion. "What . . . ?"

"Enough for him?" he asked, nodding toward Ollie, who still stood, keeping a tight hold on Bettina.

"Ohh," Josie breathed, comprehending with a sinking heart. Somehow she had always imagined Whitewater taking care of all the unpleasant details of any potential conflict. Whitewater seemed to feel certain he could handle Lucas and Willis. But there was no time for any real plan, and he was entrusting the menace Ollie presented to her hands.

"Sneak up behind him," Whitewater ordered softly, his face adamant. "Don't let him see you. Don't let him hear you. Then as soon as you see me in the open, let him have it. Understand me? I'm depending on you."

Before she knew what was happening, he kissed her lightly on the mouth. And then he was gone. He moved away from Josie as silently as a shadow, disappearing from her side as if he'd never been there. She was alone.

Stunned, she slipped her bedroll off and spread it out with trembling hands. She took out her medical kit, withdrew a hypodermic needle and a vial of immobilizing agent. Gritting her teeth, she willed herself to stop shaking as she filled the syringe with a large-enough dose to stop Ollie in his tracks. She closed the kit and, with mechanical movements, fastened it to her belt. Then she edged westward toward where Ollie and Bettina stood, praying the big man wouldn't move.

But Ollie did move. He stepped toward the landing strip, once, twice. Josie's heart seemed to die in her chest. But, she realized, numb with fear, he had simply moved farther west along the grove, the better to see Lucas and Willis leave. He still held onto Bettina. Josie began to move through the bamboo toward him. She prayed to be as silent as Whitewater.

She reached the grove behind Ollie and Bettina only to find the huge man had moved farther into the open. She examined the distance between them. She would have to move at least twelve feet into the clearing to reach him. Suddenly twelve feet seemed like an infinite and impossible distance. She stopped, her pulses thudding like funereal drums.

By standing on tiptoe and peering to the west, she could just make out Lucas and Willis as they approached the edge of the airstrip. She didn't dare make a move until Whitewater did. She could not afford to alert the other two men with any action. And she knew she could not surprise Ollie unless he was distracted by whatever Whitewater did.

She stood in the shadows, waiting, listening to the beat of her heart. Ollie took another step away from her into the clearing. She cursed silently. He stood in profile to her, so that if he turned his head but slightly when she began to move, he would see her. She bit her lip and gave a wordless curse.

Moon Flower made a peculiarly mournful sound and rubbed restlessly against the bars of her cage. Josie swallowed, trying to make the hard lump in her throat go away. The earth seemed to move beneath her, and she didn't know if there was an actual ground tremor or simply the shaking of her knees. She swallowed again. She watched the two men moving leisurely toward the hidden plane.

And then, suddenly, there were three men. Whitewater stood before the two of them, his rifle up. He had appeared as if by magic, and even from where she stood, Josie could tell he seemed to have the peculiar, grim, one-cornered smile on his face.

Ollie was saying something to Bettina, laughing unpleasantly down at her. He hadn't seen Whitewater's entrance. Josie should have made her move then, but she stood paralyzed, waiting to see if Whitewater would be all right.

"Hello," she heard him say. His quiet voice echoed with an eerie clarity across the clearing. "Put your hands up. Straight up."

Lucas froze. The small man named Willis took an involuntary step backward. Then he, too, seemed stuck to the earth. Willis's hands shot upward. "Man, I never knew it'd go this far," Willis said desperately. "I'm surrendering, man. Look, look, my hands are up. I'm glad you're here. This guy's crazy, man. He was going to get us all killed. The panda, too."

"That's all right, son," Whitewater murmured, looking down the sight of his rifle. "Just take it easy."

Move! Josie's mind commanded, but her body refused to obey. She knew Whitewater was depending on her. She had to attack, yet she was unsure she could. Besides, she was riveted by watching Lucas. She was afraid to move until she knew Whitewater had Lucas safely in hand. Lucas was more treacherous than a hundred men like Ollie.

"Who are you?" Lucas asked Whitewater petulantly. His question was half growl, half whine. He was reaching for his gun.

"Don't make me hurt you, kid," Whitewater warned.

Josie held her breath. Ollie had seen what was happening. He shoved Bettina so roughly away from him that she fell on the ground. Then he reached for his own gun.

Move! Josie's mind cried again. Ollie's hand gripped the handle of his snub-nosed gun. She flung herself out of the thicket and toward the big man. He turned to stare at her. He blinked dumbly and Josie paused for a fateful second.

Time seemed to stop. Ollie looked again across the clearing where Lucas was slowly reaching for his own gun, daring Whitewater to shoot. Ollie drew his weapon with surprising swiftness and wheeled suddenly toward the panda pen. "Everybody stop!" he yelled, his deep voice shaking in panic. "Everybody stop right now. Or I kill it. I swear I'll kill it!"

Ollie held the automatic in both hands and leveled it at Moon Flower. Josie remained rooted midway between cover and Ollie. She looked first at Moon Flower, who still paced innocently in her cage, her beautiful masked face wistful as always. Then she looked at Whitewater, who stood frozen. He raised his rifle slightly, taking aim at Ollie.

Ollie's hands trembled. He gripped his gun more tightly. He trained it more firmly on the panda. The animal stood still now, her head cocked quizzically. Lucas, Whitewater's sight no longer trained on him, seemed to be taking hold of his own gun in slow motion.

"Josie!" cried Whitewater. "Now! Now, dammit!"

A shot rang out. Ollie shrieked as the gun spun out of his hands, flying through the air and tumbling into the red dust. Josie seemed to fly the remaining few steps between her and Ollie. She heard Bettina, who still lay on the ground, cry out her name.

She pitched herself at Ollie's back and clung like a terrier attacking a larger creature. He roared and tried to throw her off. Somehow she stayed glued to him, her

arm wrapped around his fat neck. She felt him flailing
at her and bucking like a huge draft horse. She stabbed
the needle at him. She thought she felt it connect. She
pushed the plunger, but she was not sure of anything
any longer.

He flung her off, and she went flying to the earth beside Bettina, who was weeping helplessly. Josie felt
more surprise than pain. Her breath was knocked from
her, but it hardly seemed to matter. "Run, Bettina!"
she managed to pant.

Ollie took a lumbering step toward her. He stood
above her, rage on his lumpish flaccid face. Bettina
scrambled away.

Josie raised herself on her elbow. Across the clearing, she could see Lucas in a crouch, his revolver in his
hands, aimed at Whitewater. Ollie was glaring down at
her, but all she could hear was Lucas's angry scream.

"I may die!" Lucas shrieked at Whitewater. "I may
die! But I'll take you with me, I swear. We'll both die!"

Josie saw the gun shaking in his hands as he tried to
cock the revolver.

She sensed Ollie towering over her, his hands
stretching out for her.

"Son," she heard Whitewater say in his huskiest,
most sarcastic voice, "you're not worth dying for." She
saw him draw the rifle back like a club and strike Lucas
across the temple with the barrel.

Lucas crumpled slowly and awkwardly, like a figure
in a jerking piece of film. *Whitewater's alive,* Josie
thought with a dreamy sort of contentment. *He's safe.*

But almost immediately, Ollie's great hands were on
her, fastening roughly on her shirtfront, hauling her up
toward him. She felt one dirty hand close around her

throat. He had her on her feet, but his hand was squeezing the life out of her.

Whitewater, shoot him, please, she thought. *Shoot him!*

For one impossibly clear second it came to her. Her desperate wish for Whitewater to shoot went counter to everything Josie had ever professed to believe in or stand for. She wanted him to shoot. She wanted him to use violence to stop violence. She wanted him to save her.

As she fought to pry Ollie's fingers from her throat, she groggily realized why Whitewater could not shoot. Bettina, now on her feet, was hammering ineffectually at Ollie's back. She was in the way. Her sister, by trying to save her, was going to get her killed.

Josie's world went gray at its edges. Then the edges went from gray to black, and the blackness spread and spread until it covered everything.

CHAPTER SEVEN

JOSIE WAS in Whitewater's arms. He stood above Ollie's fallen body, holding her as if she were a child. He seemed like the pivot of a dizzily moving world. The sky spun slowly around his head. Only the tightness with which he held her kept everything from whirring out of control.

She tried to speak but could not. Her throat hurt. The sound she made was a feeble croak. Somehow he managed to open his canteen and put it to her lips. "There, there, love," he soothed. "I've got you. You're fine. You're going to be just fine. Take a drink, then hang on to me."

She sipped the water, but it was hard to swallow. Her throat felt bruised. With a groan, Whitewater let the canteen fall to the ground. He pulled her more tightly to him, wrapping his arms around her. She felt as if she was enclosed in the most dependable shelter in the world.

She laid her face against the rough canvas of his bush jacket. She wound her arms around his neck and hung on to him as he had ordered. He felt so solid, so strong, so invincible, she knew he could pull the whole crazy, gyrating world together again and make it safe once more.

Tears smarted beneath her eyelids, which were squeezed tightly shut. This time she didn't try to hide her crying from him. They had been through heaven and hell together, had looked into the face of death together. What could she hide from him?

"Whitewater," she whispered hoarsely, "what happened? I'm sorry. I didn't move fast enough. I failed you. I'm sorry." She hid her face more deeply against his chest. One of his many buttoned pockets scratched her cheek.

"Josie, Josie," he murmured, his lips against her tousled auburn hair. "Someday, if there's world enough and time, I'll tell you how wonderful you were. You got him. You brought him down. He fell like a redwood tree. You had a little case of buck fever, but you recovered. Everything's fine."

"B-buck fever?" Josie asked miserably, still not able to look up at him. "I don't even know what happened."

Gently he set her on her feet. He put his arms around her and didn't make her show her tearstained face. He kept it pressed against his chest. His fingers curled gently in the tangle of her bright curls. "Can you stand?"

She nodded. She had her arms around his waist now. She leaned gratefully against him. He held her comfortingly against his hard-muscled length. His voice was low and husky in her ear.

"That's my girl. Get yourself together. Don't worry about what's over. *Buck fever* means that when the critical moment came, you froze—like a hunter with a big buck in his sight. But you got over it. I think you'd make a hunter someday—if you wanted. Want to?"

The tone of his last question was gently jesting, but Josie shuddered. "No!" she said emphatically, the word muffled against his vest. She hugged herself more tightly against him, needing his strength.

"Josie!" Bettina's plaintive voice shook Josie back to actuality. "Josie, how did you get here?" Bettina asked, then sniffed loudly. "And who's this man?"

Josie tensed in Whitewater's arms. She raised her face. Slowly she looked around. From the charmed circle of safety that was Whitewater's embrace, she took in the scene.

Bettina, her face streaked with tears, knelt, almost cowering, beside the young man named Willis. Willis, looking almost relieved, sat with his close-cropped head down. His strained face look ashamed. His hands were bound expertly and tightly, and Bettina sat close to him, as if she had become used to turning to Willis for protection.

Ollie, breathing so deeply and peacefully that he almost seemed to be sleeping, lay stretched on his stomach in the dust and weeds. His fat hands were knotted behind his back.

"I got him," Josie said weakly, looking at the huge man so inert in his drugged state. "And you . . . you got Lucas," she said wonderingly, turning her eyes up at last to Whitewater's face.

He grinned down at her, teeth white against the bronze of his face. Under the shadow of his hat brim his dark eyes were momentarily teasing. "I didn't hurt him, either—at least, not a lot." He turned his head in the direction of the airstrip. Lucas, his hands bound in front of him, was slumped against a tree trunk, still unconscious. He seemed to be nodding peacefully above hands folded in his lap. His black headband was askew. His black T-shirt was covered with dust.

The sight of him still chilled Josie through. Suddenly self-conscious because of Bettina's searching stares, she stepped slightly away from Whitewater. Her knees felt shaky. He kept one arm around her, as if to guarantee she wouldn't fall. His touch was beginning to warm her with more than a sense of security. It was hard to forget for very long how purely male was this man.

"I had to tie up a few people before I got to you," he muttered apologetically. "Your sister was there, fussing over you. She kept screaming that you were all right. She screamed quite a lot, in fact, but she managed to wrestle you away from under Sleeping Beauty there." He looked with distaste on Ollie's mountainous body.

"Josie," Bettina demanded, tears welling again in her eyes, "who *is* this man? How *did* you get here?"

Josie gazed unsteadily down at her sister. "This is Whitewater," she said, holding her hand to her aching throat. It seemed that those words ought to explain everything. His arm around her waist felt like a tingling bond that branded her as his. "We came through the mountains. Are you all right?"

"No," wailed Bettina, bursting into tears. The noise made Josie's head hurt. "But I did what you said, Josie. I took care of Moon Flower. I didn't let Lucas hurt her. He was thinking about it, he really was. By the end, I was as much his prisoner as the panda was. So was Willis. We wanted out."

Josie left the tantalizing security of Whitewater's easy embrace and knelt beside her sister. She put her arm around her. "It's all right, Bettina. It's going to be all right." Deep in her doubting heart, she hoped it was true.

"I just want to say," Willis said with terrified earnestness, "that I want it on record that I surrendered. I gave myself up willingly. I'm glad to be out of it, man. Lucas had us all like kind of hypnotized. But once we had the panda . . . I could see his ego was getting out of hand, man. He thought he could make the whole world bow down to him. Bettina definitely wanted out. And I was coming around to her view. He didn't trust us alone together. I was definitely about to get out of this mess."

"He was, Josie." Bettina nodded, looking pleadingly at her sister. "And Lucas knew it. The two of us saw through him. We wished we'd never got involved. We'd just thought we could use the panda to make the world a better place."

Josie gave Bettina a perfunctory pat on the shoulder, but stood up feeling the taste of bitterness in her mouth. Already Bettina and Willis were trying to minimize their part in the crime, to lessen their guilt. "You should never have started this craziness," she said harshly. Bettina gave a gulping sob and Willis looked more ashamed, depressed and nervous. Josie stared down at the two of them. They were not an inspiring pair.

"Come on," Whitewater said, laying his hand on Josie's slender shoulder. "Let's tranquilize the panda and get out of here. I still don't like the feel of this place."

Josie nodded. She set off toward the panda pen. Her head ached and she stumbled slightly. Whitewater caught her around the waist. "Are you all right?" he asked, his brow furrowed. Again his touch surged through her like electricity.

She nodded to signal that she was. In truth, she was worried about the panda. She had recognized Moon Flower's movements, her cries. She had seen videotapes of female pandas acting similarly. She stared through the thick bars of the animal's jerry-built cage.

Moon Flower's eerie sounds, her pacing, the way she swung her hindquarters, all gave evidence of one thing: the panda was about to become a mother.

At Josie's approach, Moon Flower moved to the other side of the pen. She looked up at her with her oddly sad black-masked eyes. Then she turned away and began to nose and paw at a pile of bamboo in the corner. She was building a nest.

Josie's chest tightened. This was the moment she had dreamed of for years. But it shouldn't be happening now. And it shouldn't be happening here.

She looked up at Whitewater who still stood by her side, keeping hold of her waist. Bettina had followed the two of them to the cage. She hobbled up beside Josie. "I'm worried about her," Bettina said, wiping her hands across her eyes. "She's acting funny. She's been like this a couple of days. The whole mountain feels funny. It's like she knows something is going to happen."

Josie glanced at the exotic beauty of the panda and then back up at Whitewater. "Something's going to happen all right," she said shortly, her eyes locking with his dark ones. "We can't move her now. I think she's going to have her baby. Everything she's doing—building the nest, her noises, her movements—says this is it. We can't chance moving her."

"She's going to have it *now*?" Bettina cried in fear. "I thought we had weeks, maybe even months. How can she have it *now*?"

Josie grasped the bars of the cage and held them tightly. "Nature," she said through clenched teeth, "isn't a great respecter of timetables."

"Well," Bettina wailed, dissolving into tears again, "What are we going to *do*? I want to go home! What are we going to *do*?"

Whitewater moved from Josie's side to Bettina's. He grasped the younger sister's arm and forced her to look up into his grim face. "First thing you're going to do is stop whining," he ordered. "You think you've got it tough? Your sister's been fighting her way through these mountains for three days to get you out of this damned mess—she's had to play Superwoman, and she's done a damned fine job of it—so stop sniveling, will you? Be an adult for once in your life and help."

Bettina's face went as pale as snow. She stared up at Whitewater as if he were the first person who had ever talked to her so. "Y-yessir," she stuttered, and tried to pull her arm away.

He held her fast with one hand. With the other he reached into one of his many pockets and pulled out a piece of nylon rope. Then he released her long enough to fish his Swiss army knife out of another pocket and saw off a length of the line. He thrust it at her. "Here," he snarled. "I wanted to get to your sister. I didn't take time to tie Lucas's feet. You want to help, go do it—and do it tightly."

"Yessir," Bettina said, with almost a yip. She took the rope gingerly and sprinted off to the side of the airstrip, where Lucas was still slumped meditatively against his tree trunk, head down, body inert.

"And when you get back," he yelled after her retreating figure, "you're going to help your sister. You're going to do exactly as she says—to the letter. Understand?"

He turned back to Josie. "Sorry," he muttered. "She gets on my nerves. Now, what do we need to do for

Moon Flower? Besides get the cigars ready to pass out?"

Josie gnawed her lower lip. She still felt slightly dazed. When Ling-Lang, the female panda in Washington, D.C., had delivered her cubs, the zoo's hospital and most sophisticated equipment stood ready—as well as a dozen vets and attendants—because Ling-Lang and her offspring were so important. The animal had been surrounded by medical experts and their assistants, but even the best of care hadn't helped. Panda breeding was infinitely difficult. The babies had not survived.

"We wait," she answered uneasily. "I've read about this. I've seen it on video. But this is the first time I've ever actually been at a birth. And I'm a zoologist, not a vet. But I know the best thing is to let nature take its course. I don't want to tranquilize her unless I have to."

The sun fled behind a cloud. A sudden chill seemed to settle on the mountain. "Hey, you people?" came Willis's voice from where he and Ollie were trussed up. "Doesn't anybody else feel there's something creepy going on here? That something funny's happening on this mountain?"

Josie was too preoccupied to answer, and Whitewater refused to bother.

"I mean, I feel like something really *weird* is going to happen, you know?" Willis almost pleaded. "Even Lucas felt it, and he's as cold-blooded as they come. We can't get any radio reception in this valley. Anything could be going to happen. A hurricane or a tidal wave or anything."

Moon Flower paced. She came near Josie and Whitewater. She stopped, her seriocomic face cocked as if she recognized Josie. She raised her round head and gave an unearthly cry, as if she were frightened and asking for help.

Oh, dear heaven, thought Josie, *please don't let her have her baby. Not now. Not after all I've been through. I'm just not ready.*

The black-and-white animal shifted her weight nervously from side to side. She tilted her head the other way, still looking sad-eyed at Josie. Again she made her plaintive sound. Josie felt her knees start to buckle. She tightened her grip on the bars.

Whitewater's arm was around her again. Once more his nearness, his presence helped galvanize her, keep her tingling with life. "Steady," he said in his husky voice. "You're in charge now. I'm here. I'll do whatever you say. But I think we'd better get this girl out of here."

"We can't," she said, shaking her head. "It's dangerous enough here. I . . . can't even think about transporting her—"

Bettina came panting up beside the two of them. "I tied his feet," she said. "I tied them really tight. He's still knocked out. He's not moving at all. What should I do now, Josie?"

Josie didn't bother to glance at her sister. Bettina sounded so childish, so eager to please, so out of touch with the seriousness of the situation.

"You're sure you tied him tight?" Whitewater demanded.

"I . . . suppose you could boil some water or something," Josie told her sister. "Find some towels." Wasn't that what people always did in the movies? She was bluffing, but she maintained a tone of authority in her voice to keep Bettina semicalm.

"Yes." Bettina nodded. "I tied him really tight. Boil water? All we have is a teakettle and a little camp stove... Maybe we should take her back to Hawaii. This isn't the best place for this to happen, you know."

"I know," Josie snapped, flaring out at her sister at last. "And what do you suppose you'd be doing about it if I hadn't come along? I said go boil some water."

Bettina bolted away, disappearing inside the dilapidated little house. Whitewater looked after her, frowning. "I'm going to check on Lucas," he informed Josie. "Something tells me I shouldn't trust that kid sister of yours to even tie a knot. Sorry."

"Don't be sorry," Josie returned. "She's got us all in a wonderful fix. Oh, Moon Flower," she finished lamely, looking at the restless panda.

"Josie," Whitewater said, putting his hands on her shoulders. He looked deeply into her eyes. "I said you're the expert now. And you are. But I really think we all ought to get off this mountain, the sooner the better."

Josie felt the warmth of his hands, the comfort of his power, but she shook her head. "I can't," she began. "I can't take the responsibility. She's far too valuable, too rare to be tossed around like—"

An enormous rolling shudder shook the earth. An indescribable roar filled the air, almost deafening Josie. The ground seemed to be full of thunder and to give a slight, yet powerful surge beneath her feet.

Josie was thrown to the grass. Whitewater hurled his body across hers in protection. He caught her in his arms and held her tightly, pulling her against his chest instinctively. Josie was aware of another shuddering of the earth beneath them, and that within the cage, Moon Flower terrified, stood on her hind legs and wailed in sheer animal fear.

This was it, Josie thought, shaken to the core. They were going to die. At least Whitewater held her in his arms, and that was something.

"Whitewater?" she breathed in panic, turning her eyes up to his wary ones. Another rumble in the ground and another keening cry from Moon Flower drowned out her beseeching voice. A terrible distant roar began to shake the eastern horizon.

Whitewater rolled so that his body shielded hers more fully. She felt his length pressed against hers, his arms inexorable about her. He bent his face close to hers. "We don't have any choice, Josie," he told her between gritted teeth. "We've got to get out of here now or take a chance on never getting out. Get the panda ready."

"But—" she began, staring up helplessly into his merciless face.

"Get her ready," he repeated, almost snarling. "We don't have any choice."

And Josie, listening to Moon Flower's cries, Bettina's screams as she stumbled from the house, and the shrieking prayers of Willis, knew that Whitewater was right.

Fingers of red mist were inching up the edges of the sky. The Mount of Cloudy Gods shook as if in pain or anger or both. They had to go now. They had no choice.

For a desperate moment she clung to Whitewater. She was afraid to let go of him. But she did.

"I'm sorry, Moon Flower," she thought, struggling to her feet and looking at the terrified panda. "I'm so sorry."

And Moon Flower, as if in answer, cried out in a voice that was almost human.

CHAPTER EIGHT

THE GHOSTLY RED FINGERS of clouds crept higher up the edges of the sky. Whitewater was across the clearing, checking the plane. Bettina had fallen to her knees, wailing. She had her hands over her ears. Josie had no time to comfort her. Willis's cries of terror further addled the welter of sound.

Josie tried to shut everything out except what needed to be done. She took another syringe and a vial of the swiftest-acting but safest drug she had from her medical kit. She filled the syringe, surprising herself with the sureness of her hands. The earth seemed to give another long, sickening tremor beneath her, but she kept her balance. She refused to think about it.

Do your job, she thought again and again, as if the words were magic. *Do your job. Take care of Moon Flower.*

The giant panda, in spite of her cuddly-looking beauty and almost childlike movements, was a large and dangerous animal. Josie could not go in the cage with Moon Flower, especially as restless and as frightened as the creature was now.

She used the same Chinese method of administering the tranquilizer that was used in the panda preserve at the Wolong Preserve in Szechwan. Tying the syringe to a long stick of bamboo with gauze, she thrust it into the cage and unceremoniously stabbed Moon Flower in the rump. The panda looked more betrayed than ever and let out a pettish yelp.

Josie watched worriedly as Moon Flower began to pace and bay unhappily again. But within moments, it seemed, the animal began to sway on her ebony feet. A minute later, she stood, head down, oblivious to the tumult around her. Drunkenly, she tried to keep her balance. Then she pitched to the ground and lay in a black-and-white heap, silent.

Josie undid the cage door and raced in. She felt the panda's heartbeat, listened to her breathing, looked at the glazed, unseeing eyes. "Be all right, girl," she begged, stroking the silvery head, fondling the black ears. "Please be all right."

She heard the engines of the plane coughing into life. Assured that Moon Flower was all right so far, Josie rose, turned and raced toward the house. She pulled the weeping Bettina to her feet. "Help me!" she demanded.

"I can't!" wailed Bettina. "Oh, Josie, I'm so scared. It's like all my mistakes are coming after me! All my sins—"

Josie shook her. "Worry about your sins later. I need your help!"

Bettina looked at her uncomprehendingly, the tears running down her face. Josie gritted her teeth, drew back her hand and slapped her sister with all her might. Her hand stung from the impact.

Bettina yelped, then stared at her, as if Josie had just appeared at that very moment. "What?" Bettina asked, like someone just waking up. Her tears stopped as if by magic. Another tremor rippled the ground beneath them, and Willis started shrieking again. *How many*

hysterical people can I cope with? Josie thought hopelessly. Thank God for Whitewater.

"Get in that house," Josie ordered her sister. "Fill
any canteens with hot water. Bring all the blankets and
towels you can find. And hurry. We have to take off."

A wind had come up suddenly. Red dust was starting
to fly. The temperature seemed to have shot up ten de-
grees. Whitewater ran back from the plane, his head low
against the wind. He put his hands on Josie's upper
arms, gripping them tightly. He bent over her, placing
his mouth near her ear. "How's the panda?" he
shouted, trying to make himself heard over the engines
of the plane, the wind, the distant rumbles of Kana-
Puma, and Willis's cries.

"She's out," Josie shouted back, her throat burning
with the effort. She gripped Whitewater's forearms
tightly. He was the only one she could count on or trust.
"But we're going to have to be careful moving her. This
really scares me, Whitewater—drugging her at a time
like this."

He nodded curtly. "You'll have to trust nature to help
you out," he said grimly. He went to Willis and began
untying his bonds. Willis hiccuped back a sob and
wiped his nose on the sleeve of his checkered shirt.

"Come on, cowboy," Whitewater rasped, hauling the
smaller man to his feet. "You're going to help me carry
a panda."

"Anything," Willis wept, grabbing Whitewater by
the front of his vest. "Just get me out of here—please!"

Whitewater knocked his hands away contemp-
tuously. "Come on," he snapped. "First the panda.
Then your friend." He nodded at the unconscious bulk
of Ollie stretched out on the ground. He seized Willis by
the shirt collar and yanked him toward the panda pen.

Josie followed. There was a large dirty piece of ply-wood in the pen. It must have been used to move the tranquilized panda when she was brought to the island. Whitewater and the terrified Willis picked up Moon Flower gingerly and wrestled her onto the sheet of wood.

"Now come on," ordered Whitewater. "Lift this board and let's carry her on that plane. Drop your end, and you'll be looking for your head on the next chain of islands."

With a groan the two men heaved the board with the panda up and bore it toward the plane, Whitewater leading. Josie trailed after then, carrying an armful of bamboo.

"There's a pen of sorts in the plane," Whitewater answered, struggling to carry the board up the steps leading into the plane. "They were too lazy to take it off, I guess." Willis almost lost his grip. "Watch it!" Whitewater snapped.

Finally the two men shouldered their heavy burden into the plane. Josie climbed the steps and looked into the plane's interior, which seemed impossibly hot and cramped. Instead of a door, the cage had one whole side that unfastened and came down. Josie opened it and spread the bamboo on its floor. She watched, chewing nervously at her lips as Whitewater managed to lift the panda from her board and place her, with a groan, into the cage.

She snapped the cage's wall back into place and fol-lowed the two men out of the plane once more. The temperature seemed to have climbed several more de-grees. The wind was higher, the cruelly blowing dust thicker. She looked at the sky, the wind whipping her hair. The dust was clouding everything, yet the sky was still visible through the first swirling layers of red and gray.

She ran toward Bettina, taking an armload of blankets from her. Grasping her sister's hand, she ran back toward the plane. Whitewater and Willis had lifted the unconscious mound that was Ollie. Whitewater had his shoulders, Willis his feet. Together the two men carried him to the plane, hanging like a bag of grain between them.

"Get up those stairs," Josie ordered, and Bettina obeyed without a murmur, disappearing inside the plane. "Get in!" yelled Whitewater over his shoulder, but Josie stood her ground stubbornly, wanting to see him and his burden safely inside.

When she didn't obey, he swore, but he was too anxious to dispose of the blubbery load of Ollie to take time to quarrel with her. He dumped his half of the big bald man inside the plane, gave the inert form one last push so that it disappeared inside, then shoved Willis aside from the stairs and came back down after Josie.

He reached for her wrist, clamped it in an iron grip and started to haul her up the stairs. "I said, *get in!*" he ordered. He made a move as if he were about to carry her aboard.

The hot wind tossed Josie's curls wildly. "Lucas!" she cried, trying to pull away from Whitewater's commanding grasp. "We can't leave Lucas!"

His face darkened. "I'll get him. You get in the plane. I don't want those other two taking off without us. Here. Take this." He pressed Lucas's revolver into her reluctant hand. He practically hoisted her up the stairs as he had done so many times on the mountain steeps. She struggled uselessly, looking back over her shoulder to make sure Lucas was all right.

She felt Whitewater's hands, one firmly on her shoulder, the other on her hip, about to push her through the doorway of the plane. Another gust of wind, stronger than any before it, made him frown all the harder.

"Get in, dammit!" he muttered.

But the sudden fright in her blue-green eyes made him suddenly freeze, then turn, following her horrified gaze.

"He's gone!" Josie cried, appalled. She stared at the tree Lucas had been slumped against. The space was empty except for the hot gusting dust. The wind was beginning to scream in the trees.

Whitewater released her, then ran toward the tree, unslinging his rifle from his shoulder. Josie followed. The nylon rope that Bettina had used to tie Lucas's feet fluttered against a clump of weeds. He had escaped.

A crude path of freshly broken bamboo showed his route. He was heading down the mountain, the way they had come. Whitewater's head cocked, as if he could somehow hear Lucas in the distance, crashing through the undergrowth. He raised the rifle.

Josie grabbed the barrel with both hands, dragging it down. "No!" she screamed against the ranting wind.

Whitewater looked at her angrily. "I had a glimpse of him," he gritted out. "I could have winged him, brought him down. The only way I can get him now is to go after him. And if I go after him, none of us may get out of here."

Josie stared up at him, the dilemma sinking into her brain. Behind her the plane's engines roared and coughed, roared and coughed. The wind howled more shrilly. The sky grew darker. The dust flew more thickly.

"Choose," he ordered, staring down at her. "What do you want me to do? Get everybody off this island now—or try to save Lucas?"

Josie's hand was on his arm now, but she seemed to have no feeling in her body. She listened numbly as Kana-Puma gave another monstrous rumble in the distance.

"I can't choose," she whispered, her answer lost in the rising wind.

But he heard her. "I can," he said implacably. His arm circled her waist and he practically carried her back to the plane.

"But we can't leave him here!" she objected, looking in disbelief at the clearing, empty now of life.

"Get in the plane," growled Whitewater. "Take care of the panda. This is my decision."

Bettina and Willis helped pull the resisting Josie inside. "Get in, Josie," begged Bettina.

"Man, you are really lucky I didn't try to take off without you," Willis said, shaking his head nervously as Whitewater entered the plane. Willis was sitting in the pilot's seat, as if ready to start taxiing down the decaying little runway.

Whitewater hauled him out of the seat and deposited him with a thump on the floor of the plane. "No," he snarled, taking the controls. "*You're* lucky you didn't try to take off without me. You'd be in more pieces than a jigsaw puzzle. Tie him up, Josie."

He reached into his pockets, extracted the rope and his Swiss Army knife and tossed them to her. She caught them automatically. Mechanically she obeyed him. Willis was weak, but he was treacherous. She struggled to saw off a length of rope.

Willis sat on the floor, holding his wrists out toward her, ready to be cooperative. At last Josie hacked off a section of rope and knotted it around his proffered hands. The plane was bucking as it tried to lift off the runway against the wind.

She glanced at the cockpit. Outside the sky was growing darker, more stained with the swirling red dust. The plane gave a sickening pitch and Bettina shrieked and hid her face.

Whitewater seemed to do something swift and violent at the controls. The plane tilted, dived, then shot up. It rolled slightly, bucked again and then somehow straightened out. They were clear of the rumbling earth, heading toward the churning edge of the cloud.

Josie stared in exhaustion at the knots she had managed to tie around Willis's wrists. It looked as if she had been trying to tether an elephant.

"I think we're going to make it," Bettina said in awe, clasping her hands on Josie's shoulders. "Josie, I think he's actually going to get us out of here!"

Josie looked gratefully at Whitewater's wide back. He was concentrating completely on reaching the edge of the cloud. She looked at Bettina, whose pale face shone with relief.

"Bettina," Josie said, her own face feeling wooden and expressionless, "don't you realize? We didn't get Lucas. He got away. He's down there somewhere."

Far below them they heard a tremendous roar. The plane pitched wildly, but then hit air that was relatively clear. Beneath, receding from the plane, the island was disappearing in a thickening cloak of dust. The cloak was rent by a flicker of flame, a rising column of smoke. Kana-Puma had erupted.

"I said he's down there," Josie repeated bitterly. "Your friend. He's trapped."

Bettina looked unfazed. She stared at Josie with petulant innocence. "He's not my friend," she said, childishly. "I don't care. He deserves whatever happens to him."

"Bettina!" Josie cried, horrified at her sister's coldness.

Willis was nodding philosophically, as if he, too, simply dismissed the fate of the man he had so lately called his leader. And Whitewater had already proved he didn't care what happened to Lucas. Nobody cared. Perhaps Josie shouldn't, either, but her heart felt leaden, lifeless. Was she the only one of them who cared what happened to a fellow human being?

"I wonder," she said, her face ashen, "if he can survive." She spoke almost to herself.

The only answer was the roar of the plane's churning engines. At last Whitewater said, "It's his problem, Josie. Not yours."

She wished she could believe that. Perhaps if she had not been so blind, so careless, so foolishly eager to help Bettina, none of this would have happened. Moon Flower would never have been kidnapped, and Lucas would not now be trapped by the fearsome power of Kana-Puma.

"Uh," said Willis helpfully, scratching his ear with the knotted rope on his wrists. "Excuse me for interrupting your thoughts—" he paused delicately "—but I think something is happening to your panda."

Josie looked at him, blinking hard. Then she looked at Moon Flower, lying drowsily on the floor of the cage. The black-and-white fur of her side was rippling in a rhythmic wave.

"Oh, no," breathed Josie. She felt dizzy all over. "She's going to have it. Here. Now."

She unlatched the cage and laid one hand on Moon Flower's rounded side. Moon Flower, too groggy to be frightened, gave Josie a weak bleat of welcome. "Whitewater," Josie called, her voice sounding thin in her ears. "Fly this thing very straight. We're about to have a baby."

He didn't look at her. His attention focused on the controls. "We're also about to have some air turbulence. Hang on. It's like we're hitting a tidal wave of air. And I'm going to have to take the long way out of here to avoid the worst of it. We're going to have to watch the fuel to the last inch."

She barely heard him. She was too busy monitoring the panda's breathing. For fear of harming the imminent birth, Josie had not administered that great a dose of the drug, and now it appeared Moon Flower was starting to come around, perhaps stirred to consciousness by her contractions. When the plane began to buck again, Josie forced herself not to notice, although Bettina kept clinging to the back of her seat and squeaking in fright.

Moon Flower whimpered, perplexity in her dazed eyes. "I guess we're in nature's hands now," Josie murmured, stroking the panda's head soothingly.

"We always are, Red," Whitewater muttered back, in his husky voice. He maneuvered the plane through another rise and drop. "We always are."

"Uh," Willis put in, not looking very well, "this plane is pitching around a lot. And I, uh, I've never seen anything born before, and I'm feeling kind of funny...."

"Then don't look," growled Whitewater. "Let the lady do her job. Let both ladies do their jobs."

"Whitewater," Josie said, "I wish you could help me." The panda was panting now, her half-open eyes more puzzled than ever.

"I am helping you," he answered grimly. "I'm keeping this plane in the air. So far."

Bettina kept her face hidden against the back of her seat, and Willis had lain down on the floor at Bettina's feet. "I mean," Josie said to Whitewater, wiping the perspiration from her brow, "I wish you could give me some moral support. Or something."

The plane rolled, gave a lurch and straightened out again. Josie did her best to hold Moon Flower steady and keep her from being thrown about. "Let's sing," Whitewater said. It was more order than request.

"Right," Josie agreed, spreading the blankets around Moon Flower to cushion her. "We'll sing."

She forgot that Whitewater knew only one song and couldn't sing very well. She forgot everything except that he was there with her, working with her in spirit. As usual, she was depending on him.

WHITEWATER HAD TO FLY so far west to avoid the tumultuous air generated by Kana-Puma that the baby panda was born outside the territory of the United States, over international waters. It was born during what seemed to Josie to be the three-hundredth time they had sung "Waltzing Matilda."

It was a male, born, in fact, during the line that goes, "Once a jolly swagman sat beside a billabong." The cub was alive, and Josie wept in relief. She immediately christened the newcomer Billabong, and called him Billy for short.

Bettina, still fearful, kept her face hidden, and Willis, slightly green, groaned on the floor, seeming in far worse shape than Moon Flower herself, who did not yet quite realize that she was a mother. The panda was far more conscious than Ollie, who snored loudly in the very rear of the plane. Whitewater had rolled him there for ballast.

Just before the cub's birth, Whitewater had turned the plane southeast, heading back toward Hawaii. If they couldn't make the island of Oahu, he said, they certainly ought to be able to make Kauai, the northernmost of the large islands. The winds had shifted. They were free from the shock waves of Kana-Puma.

Josie tenderly rubbed the cub with a towel warmed with water from the canteen. Billy was not a prepossessing baby: no bigger than a newborn kitten, he weighed only a fraction of a pound. His head was flat, his eyes were sealed shut, and his little pink body was nearly naked, covered only by the haziest sprinkling of silvery fuzz. He had a rather unpleasant-looking little tail that would disappear as he grew older. The distinctive black markings would not appear for a week. He looked like a large, bald, bobtailed rat. To Josie, he was beautiful.

Billy had only enough strength to pipe a shrill baby cry. But Moon Flower, using paw and mouth, moved the cub to her chest, and he began to suckle with enthusiasm. Josie gave a sigh of relief. She kept close watch on the mother panda so she would not roll on the cub or accidentally injure him in any way.

"I wonder what his nationality is?" Josie said, patting Moon Flower's flank and watching Billy fall asleep as he fed. "His parents come from China but are residents of the States. He was born over international waters to the Australian national anthem.''

'' 'Waltzing Matilda' isn't the Australian national anthem,'' Whitewater said, flying through dark clouds once more as they headed toward Honolulu. ''It's just Australian.'' He sounded oddly moody. He was probably as exhausted as she was. But she glowed with happiness anyway.

''Well,'' Josie went on, ''maybe it all just proves he's a citizen of the world. The pandas really should belong to everyone.''

She smiled down at Billabong's ugly little form. Tiredly she wiped a damp strand of hair from her eyes and glanced around the crowded plane. Ollie was crammed into the rear section. Moon Flower's open cage took up much of the remaining space. Bettina sat crouched in the one passenger seat, her face still buried in the back cushion. Willis was huddled at her feet.

''Josie?'' Bettina lifted her face. It was pale, and her eyes were swollen. ''The baby's really all right?''

''He's all right,'' Josie said, nodding with contentment. She could hardly believe it herself. Nature had come through, had somehow triumphed.

''And we're really going to make it to Hawaii?'' Bettina asked. She slipped off her seat and crouched beside her sister, cramping up to fit in the small space.

Josie smiled as Moon Flower's black paw moved up in an instinctive gesture to protect her cub. She closed the door, then leaned back, resting against one of the empty auxiliary tanks. ''We're going to make it to Hawaii,'' she said, and looked at Bettina's troubled, freckled young face.

''The baby isn't very pretty, is he?'' Bettina asked, her voice trembling.

"He is to me," Josie answered gently. "He's the prettiest baby I ever saw."

Bettina turned to her sister so that their eyes met. "Josie," she whispered, her chin quivering, "what do you think they'll do to me? Will they put me in jail?"

Josie could not fight down the surge of warmth and pity she felt for the unhappy girl. "I don't think so," she answered softly. "You wanted to get away from Lucas. You called for help. We wouldn't have made it if you hadn't been brave enough to call."

"I tried to do the right thing, Josie. I really did," Bettina said quaveringly. She hid her face against Josie's shoulder.

Josie put her arm around her sister and hugged her tightly. "You'll be all right, Bettina," she assured the girl, who was crying softly now. She squeezed her again. "Whitewater says if you give evidence against Lucas, the authorities might not press any charges at all. And he ought to know—his brother's a lawyer. Isn't that right, Whitewater?"

She held the weeping Bettina and waited for Whitewater's answer and assurance. But he said nothing. He was talking in a low voice on the plane's radio. Josie sighed and smoothed her sister's tangled pale red hair.

"Anyway, that's what he said. Probably nobody's going to do anything to you, Bettina. Just cooperate, understand?"

Bettina nodded. Awkwardly she sat up straight and wiped her eyes. "I'll tell them everything," she said. "It was Lucas's idea. I made the mistake of writing to him. I told him I was working at the zoo. He already knew you were involved with the pandas. He hatched this crazy plot—to hold Moon Flower for ransom. At first it was going to be a simple protest—you know, for animal rights, to save the whales and everything. I thought even you wouldn't really object, Josie, as long as you knew Moon Flower would be all right."

Josie felt herself going cold all over, but Bettina wiped her eyes again and went on, "Lucas knew about the mountain," she said with a sniff, "because one of his stepfathers worked for Trans-Pacific Foods in the Honolulu office. He'd been there a bunch of times when he was small. He remembered the way, the airstrips and everything."

Josie felt even colder, thinking of Lucas. She wondered if he were still alive. Now that they were almost safe she felt a certain pity for him, twisted and self-important as he was.

"Lucas met Ollie in Boston," Bettina continued, looking down at Moon Flower and Billabong. "Ollie thought Lucas was brilliant. He'd do anything that Lucas said. Lucas used him for all the rough and hard work—like handling Moon Flower."

Bettina shuddered slightly. "And Willis, Willis was the electrical genius. Lucas was the philosophical genius and the great pilot and all that, but it was Willis who figured out a way to break into the zoo and the panda house. I think he did it almost as a sort of game, a challenge. Once we got Moon Flower and Lucas started going so strange, Willis didn't like what was going on any better than I did."

"I want it noted," Willis gurgled miserably from his sickbed on the floor, "that I surrendered willingly. I didn't resist. I cooperated with my captors. I saw the error of my ways and did my best to make restitution." He ceased his self-defense, interrupted by a groan of nausea.

Josie felt a bit ill herself. She kept her arm around Bettina and hugged her close again. She personally didn't care if Willis spent the next six thousand years in the darkest pit of the darkest prison in the world, and Ollie could spend them with him, plus another six thousand just for good measure.

"I think Lucas would have killed her," Bettina admitted in a choked voice, "as a symbol. He was going to ask for something impossible—like an end to all wars and all weapons thrown away. Something that couldn't be done. And then he'd kill the panda to show the world how evil and crazy it was. But it was Lucas who was evil, Josie. He wanted everybody to bow to him. He wanted to punish the whole world."

Josie shivered. "Don't think about it," she soothed. She could not bear to think about it herself. She had what she'd come for—her sister and Moon Flower and Moon Flower's baby, and now they were heading home. Or at least toward the first stop on the way home.

She tried not to think about what awaited them. Dr. Hazard would be delighted to have Moon Flower back. He would be deeply thankful that the cub was alive and well. But Josie had no illusions about getting her job back. What her future held was a mystery, veiled in clouds thicker than those that darkly cloaked Ra-Koma.

She tried not to look at Whitewater, who still spoke softly into the mouthpiece of the radio and listened carefully on the earphones. She could not depend on him to make sense of her future for her. She had depended on him for too much already.

She loved him, she supposed wearily. It wasn't an infatuation and it wasn't merely gratitude mixed with the excitement of adventure. She loved him now, and she would love him ten years from now, and if she lived forever, she would love him that long, too.

Did he care for her at all? She thought he did. She hoped so. But he had told her he was not a man to settle down. It didn't matter. If he wanted her another week, another month, she was his, and that was that. She was his for as long as he wanted, and when he didn't want her any longer, she would quietly go away, but she would still be his.

She wrapped her arm more tightly around her sister, who had collapsed in worry and exhaustion against her shoulder. "You'll be all right," Josie assured her softly. "You'll be fine." Surely, she thought hopefully, Whitewater was right. The authorities would spare Bettina when they knew she had informed on Lucas, when they knew she would tell the whole story of what had happened.

There was a change in atmosphere, somehow, in the cramped cabin of the little plane. Josie raised her head to peer out the window. She stretched, her muscles protesting. In the distance, as if in a fog, she could see the first pinpoints of light that signaled Honolulu. They were almost there, almost safe.

"Here," she said to Bettina, straightening her sister's tousled hair, "tidy yourself up. We want you to look good when we land—nice and respectable, so everybody knows you're one of the good guys, all right? Come on, Bettina, hold your head up. You've done fine. You kept Moon Flower safe. And you called me so we could come and get you."

"You really think they won't do anything to me?" Bettina asked, tugging ineffectually at her crumpled shirt and shorts. Her voice was childlike, pleading for reassurance.

"Why should they?" Josie asked, wiping the dirty tear streaks from her sister's face. She patted Bettina's pale cheek. "You're practically a heroine."

"I tried to do the right thing," Bettina repeated, "once I realized. Honest, I did."

"I know." Josie nodded. Again, Bettina laid her face against Josie's shoulder and Josie held her close. Everyone was going to be fine, she told herself. Everyone was going to be safe. And she would worry about Whitewater then, after he'd gotten them all there. After he'd taken them the whole way.

She felt the plane descending. Her ears rang. Moon Flower stirred uneasily, shaking her head in her sleep. Josie bent to make sure Billabong was all right.

"Have you called for an ambulance and some zoo people for these two?" she asked Whitewater, raising her voice so she could be heard above the noise of the plane's engines.

She turned and looked over her shoulder at him. His only reply was an abrupt nod. The plane was descending sharply now.

She smoothed Moon Flower's black-and-white coat again. "I suppose," she said, her voice strained, "you've called the authorities, too."

There was a silence. "Yes," he said at last. She felt the plane banking slightly, held her breath and felt the wheels lowering, the impact of them hitting the tarmac. They were home. They were safe. At last.

Josie leaned back again, turning so she could see him. She draped her arm protectively once more around Bettina's neck. "Whitewater," she said, her voice strained, "I don't want to turn Bettina over to a bunch of strangers after all this. I just can't."

"You won't," he muttered, not looking at her. He was staring at the runway and listening to his headphones. His reply to her seemed almost absentminded, cold. "Have to turn her over to strangers, that is."

"Good," she said, and leaned back, her heart beating hard. The plane coasted to a standstill. Already she could hear the sirens: the ambulance, she supposed, coming for Moon Flower and Billabong. And a police escort for the ambulance most likely. And the authorities. To take away Willis and the still-drugged Ollie. But her sister, for whom she had journeyed so far, would stay free, she prayed.

It seemed odd, the plane being still. The sirens grew louder. She could see the reflection of flashing red and blue lights on the interior of the plane. They danced over the dozing Moon Flower and her cub.

Whitewater arose. He went to the door and opened it. He jerked Willis to his feet and practically thrust him out the door. Willis, still feeling sick, staggered. Whitewater growled something unintelligible, then pushed him unceremoniously down the steps. Willis practically stumbled into the arms of two waiting men in suits. FBI agents or plainclothesmen, Josie thought nervously.

Attendants were opening the back doors of an ambulance, pulling out gurneys and stretchers. The spinning red light washed over them. Josie stood, readying herself to help them. She kept her arm tightly around Bettina, and helped her to stand. They could not quite straighten. Whitewater stood on the top step as Josie started to steer Bettina outside to the clean open air.

"Where are you going?" he asked Josie harshly. His voice was surprisingly grim. His hat was off, and the

Hawaiian breeze, smelling slightly smoky, tossed his dark hair.

"To help the zoo attendants," she said, looking up at his stony features. "And to take care of my sister."

"I'm sorry," he said, putting his hand on Bettina's wrist. "You're not going anywhere. You're under arrest." A muscle in his jaw twitched. A nerve jerked in his temple. "Both of you," he said.

"What?" Josie asked, not comprehending. She stared up at him, his shadowed face, his tossing dark hair. Didn't he understand? She had a panda to take care of, and a cub. They were infinitely valuable and she must stay with them. And her sister, who was also infinitely valuable, needed her, too. She had come all this way in hopes her sister would not be arrested.

"You're both under arrest," he repeated implacably. He reached into one of his countless pockets. He pulled out a slim wallet and flipped it open before Josie's puzzled eyes.

"Aaron Whitewater, special appointed agent. For this case. Federal Bureau of Investigation. Bettina Talbott, you're under arrest for grand larceny, interstate transportation of stolen property and attempted extortion."

Josie felt Bettina starting to crumple beside her. She clutched her sister tighter. *"What?"* she demanded as Bettina sagged, weeping silently against her.

"I'm sorry," he repeated mechanically. The red and blue lights chased shadows across his face. The sirens were like an insane chorus behind his words. "And you, Josie Allen Talbott, are under arrest for withholding information from federal authorities."

The evening breeze held the tang of the ocean and the faint scent of volcanic smoke. She stared at him, open-mouthed. The runway lights, the tower lights behind him, seemed to blur crazily.

"You brought me all this way," she whispered in disbelief, "to arrest me?" Her teeth were on edge. She hugged her sister closer to her. "Whitewater, you're some kind of bastard. You really are."

"Josie," he began. "It was my job."

"Your *job*?" she said, almost sick with shock. She glared at him. She gladly would have killed him.

He said nothing. And she could say nothing more. Another two men in suits were on the stairs, crowding her and Bettina, pulling them apart. One slipped handcuffs onto Bettina's wrist. The second snapped an identical pair on Josie.

"Welcome to Hawaii, miss," the man said to Josie, smirking at her helpless expression. "Or as we say here in the islands, aloha."

Aloha, Josie thought bitterly. No wonder Whitewater had been able to leave Lucas so coldly, so calmly. He was nothing but a mercenary. Perhaps in a way he had been kinder to Lucas than to her. He'd left him to an easier fate than the one he'd bestowed on Josie. Her heart felt like a poison stone within her. Aloha, indeed.

"Josie," he said from the top of the steps, his voice hesitant, "I owe you an explanation. And you owe me a hearing. It's all—"

"Don't speak to me, Whitewater," she hissed. She couldn't bear to look at him. "Not now. Not ever."

Whitewater followed them down the steps. The agent who had Josie opened the back door of a long black car.

"The women don't need cuffs," Whitewater growled to the man. "Take the cuffs off."

"Steady, Whitewater," the agent said with an unpleasant smile. "Your work is over. We'll handle them from here."

"Josie!" Bettina cried in terror. The agent who had her imprisoned was making her get in the back of another anonymous car. The two women were being separated. Bettina's pale face, her wide eyes, were full of panic.

Whitewater spoke grimly out of the side of his mouth. "I said," he muttered as the other agent made Josie get into the car, "she doesn't need to be cuffed. They don't need to be separated, either. This woman isn't dangerous— Look, I want to go with her. I promised her that she wouldn't have to—"

"You had no right to promise her anything," the agent snapped, looking up at the larger man, "It's my job from here on out. You'll be debriefed later."

"Dammit!" Whitewater's voice was harsh, but Josie could not see his face. The agent crowded into the back seat beside her, pulling the door shut. He favored her with his smug smile and raised his hand so the handcuffs glittered in the changing lights. She was in custody. Ruined. Betrayed by Whitewater. The man she had trusted with her life.

CHAPTER NINE

BY AND LARGE, Hawaii was glamorous, but there were exceptions. One of them was the small, nearly bare interrogation room in the headquarters of the Honolulu police department, where Josie was held and questioned for almost four hours.

She refused to talk without a lawyer present. One was produced immediately, almost as if by magic. He was a medium-sized man with a receding hairline and a dashing little mustache and goatee. His name was Mr. Suehiro.

The expensive cut of Mr. Suehiro's suit, the intelligence gleaming from his eyes, the expertise with which he advised Josie, made her suspect that he was no ordinary attorney. She did not question how she had been lucky enough for him to come to her aid. She simply accepted his presence with gratitude. Mr. Suehiro seemed like the first good thing to happen to her in almost two weeks.

Before midnight, miraculously, he was ushering her out of police headquarters and into his car, a snappy little red sports model. The pleasant breezes of the tropical night around them made the interlude in the police station seem like an unlikely dream.

"I don't know where you came from," Josie told Mr. Suehiro, "but I'm glad you showed up. I hope my sister is as lucky."

"Thank you. Your sister is precisely as lucky," Mr. Suehiro answered, eyeing the traffic with competitive relish. "I will also represent her."

"You?" Josie asked in surprise. "Then you'd better go to her. She needs you far more than I do. And—" she paused in confusion, looking around at the lights of downtown Honolulu "—I don't even know where to go." She almost laughed. "I don't have any place to go. No place to sleep. You should have left me at the police station."

Josie looked at the dapper Mr. Suehiro in bewilderment. She did not even have a purse. She had nothing except the clothes on her back.

"Your sister is in the capable hands of my assistant, Hiram Rizal, who won't allow her to talk to authorities until I've had a chance to speak with her," Mr. Suehiro informed her. "I am taking you to one of the hotels on Waikiki Beach. Your needs will be taken care of."

The bright lights of the lively Waikiki section dazzled Josie, making her feel dizzy and not quite real. "I can't afford a hotel," she murmured grimly.

"It has been taken care of," Mr. Suehiro replied airily.

"Taken care of?" Josie demanded, looking at him in bewilderment. "By whom? I don't know anybody here."

He glanced at her calmly. "You have your friends, Miss Talbott. That's all I'm allowed to say at this point. Please don't question me further. You'll be staying at the hotel for at least a week. Authorities will want to talk to you again."

People in bright clothes and leis milled along the sidewalks of the Waikiki strip; lights sparkled and shone. Josie frowned at it all slightly, as if she were seeing someone else's dream. Her heart still felt leaden, weighted with the crushing heaviness of Whitewater's betrayal.

She pushed thoughts of him from her mind. She hated him, and would not allow the venom of his treachery to spread any further through her system. If she did, it would paralyze her, numb her forever. She fought the memory of him as one might fight a dangerous opponent.

"What's going to happen to my sister?" she asked softly, as Mr. Suehiro pulled up at the entrance of the very hotel she and Whitewater had stayed at before they left for the Kali Yin Islands.

"Your sister will be fine, I am sure," he stated, parking the car. He got out, came to the passenger side, opened her door and offered her his elbow to escort her inside.

Josie, tired, bedraggled, her clothes smudged with volcanic dust, felt eyes following her across the luxurious lobby as the spotless Mr. Suehiro squired her to the desk. She knew that her dark red curls were in a tumble, that her boots looked as if she had hiked halfway across hell and that she smelled of panda. She didn't care.

Mr. Suehiro acquired her key, took her to the elevators. "How soon before they release Bettina?" she persisted. "They will release her, won't they?"

The doors of an elevator swept softly open. A well-dressed man and a silken gowned woman gazed down their noses at Josie as they swept out of the elevator and she hobbled in, Mr. Suehiro still gallantly holding her elbow.

"I am certain Bettina will be released soon." Mr. Suehiro nodded confidently. "I will have her put in my own custody if it will make matters any easier. You are free to come and go as you wish, but you must not leave the island until you are so advised. And, of course, you are to say nothing of what has happened."

The elevator doors opened with a sigh, and he led her down the hall to a door that seemed familiar in a ghostly sort of way. He unlocked it. She stepped inside. Again she frowned, rubbed her forehead in confusion.

This had been her room, she realized slowly. The few belongings she hadn't taken to the island were here. She had been sure she had left them in Whitewater's custody. But her azure suit hung in the closet, her plain white nightgown was laid out in readiness for her on the turned-down bed. It looked as if it had been laundered and ironed. Her purse was set neatly on the table by a vase of flowers.

"I don't understand this—" she began, but Mr. Suehiro cut her off with the wave of one manicured hand.

"You have more important things to think of. And more important things to do, such as rest. Don't trouble your head about this. I'll be in touch with you tomorrow morning."

Josie nodded. She ached to get out of her dirty clothes, to relax in the deep luxury of the bath. But too many questions surged and eddied in her weary mind.

Mr. Suehiro swung open the doors of the room's teakwood bar. "You look," he said suavely, "like a woman who drinks white wine. But tonight I suggest brandy. You haven't had a white wine sort of day. Sit down, sit down, my dear."

Josie sank into a cushioned rattan chair by the draped sliding doors that led to the balcony. "Mr. Suehiro," she said, a lump in her throat, "I have to ask you about

Mr. Whitewater. Does he have anything to do with all this?''

She nodded to indicate the room, the hotel, Mr. Suehiro himself.

He shrugged. "Mr. Whitewater? Not that I know of," he replied smoothly. He handed her the glass, filled to the brim. "Here, take this."

Reluctantly she took the glass. She tasted its fiery contents. The burning liquid was almost pleasurable. "How did he know?" she asked bitterly, not looking at Suehiro. "How did the FBI know? Was I really foolish enough to call up one of their agents to help me?"

Mr. Suehiro sat in the other rattan chair. "As I understand it, Miss Talbott," he said carefully, "your phone was tapped. The Bureau heard your call to Mr. Whitewater. His work has taken him to trouble spots before. The Bureau has used him as an operative from time to time. In emergencies. This was such an emergency. They asked him to cooperate when you arrived. He agreed."

"He agreed," Josie repeated tonelessly. She took another sip of the searing liquor, grimacing as if it were medicine.

Mr. Suehiro nodded and rose. "If you were correct and the panda actually had been taken to the Kali Yins, who would be better qualified to find it than Mr. Whitewater? Or to ensure its welfare better than yourself? You see, inadvertently, you offered the Bureau the solution to a very knotty problem. A problem, by the way, everyone still wishes kept quiet for the time being. The less publicity the better. None of us wishes a repetition of this unfortunate incident."

He extended his hand to bid her farewell. "You may call the Honolulu Zoo tomorrow about your panda.

Ask for Dr. Kokua. From what I have heard, both mother and child are doing fine. Congratulations for a job well done.''

Josie shook his hand shyly, conscious of her disheveled state. She started to rise to see him to the door, but he shook his head. "I will let myself out, Miss Talbott," he stated softly. "Good evening. And don't worry. I'm sure the government has no intention of pressing any charges against you. You acted under duress—threats from Lucas Panpaxis. And you conducted yourself bravely and in full cooperation with their agent, Mr. Whitewater. In fact, under the circumstances, you conducted yourself better than he. The way in which he violated his professionalism certainly leaves the Bureau embarrassed. They won't wish to tangle with you, Miss Talbott. Rest assured.''

Josie looked at the natty and dignified Mr. Suehiro in surprise. "What?" she asked, puzzled. "What violation of his professionalism?" Whitewater was a traitor, she thought coldly, but he had been a perfectly professional traitor; she had never suspected him for a moment.

Mr. Suehiro had his hand on the doorknob. He stared tactfully at the floor. "I mean," he said quietly, "that Mr. Whitewater became . . . your lover. He should not have done this. You were, as I said, under tremendous duress. It was not his place to make advances to you. Especially when you seemed to have no choice but to be indebted to him.''

Josie almost dropped her glass. She gaped open-mouthed at Mr. Suehiro. "My *lover*?" she asked, horrified. "He said he was my lover? That's a lie! A filthy lie!''

Mr. Suehiro gave a little half bow of deference. "It's all right, Miss Talbot," he said soothingly. "I'm your lawyer. You need hide nothing from me. I'll talk to you tomorrow."

Quietly he opened the door, and quietly he slipped outside, shutting it behind him. Josie set her drink on the table and stared at the closed door. She felt her face burning with a heat that was not a product of the brandy. Her chest, too, flamed. So Whitewater hadn't been content just to lie to her and betray her, had he? He had to boost his miserable masculine ego the final notch and claim he'd made love to her, as well.

She rose blindly, looking for something to break. She wanted to hurl her glass at the mirror, to pick up the china ashtray from the nightstand and smash it against the sliding doors. She wanted to erupt like Kana-Puma, to lay waste her surroundings, to let her anger destroy.

But the surroundings were not truly hers. They were the hotel's. She didn't own enough in the room to break. She opened the glass doors and stepped out onto her little balcony. She gripped the white wrought-iron balcony and stared into the night.

Tonight she could barely make out the silhouette of Diamond Head in the distance. A haze hung in the air, filtering the moonlight, making the stars all but invisible. The sea sighed and crashed on the pale beach, sighed and crashed endlessly.

Lovers, she thought resentfully. He didn't want to leave her so much as a scrap of pride. She pressed her hands against her eyes. She wanted to cry, to stand in the warm breeze, listen to the sound of the sea and weep. But she couldn't; no tears would come. It was as if he had killed even her power to cry.

She was so wounded and angry that her head hurt. *It's all right,* she told herself. He used you. But you used him, too. You got Bettina back and Moon Flower back, and Billy's fine. What difference does Whitewater make? None.

She shook her head, turned helplessly and went back inside. The draperies billowed behind her. Whitewater's final selfish lie about making love to her was the last, humiliating flourish of his duplicity. She would hate him as long as she lived.

Again she wished she could break something. But the wish was hollow. The most important thing she owned was already broken. It was her heart, and she had nothing to do with its being shattered. Whitewater had done it all, and had done a good job, one that would last. With his easy smile and easy lies.

For the first time she noticed the fresh flowers on the table. The white blooms were so exotic she could not say exactly what they were: some sort of extremely large and ornate orchids. The envelope propped against them was written in a bold hand she instinctively recognized: Whitewater's.

She picked up the envelope. She did not open it. She took the delicate white blossoms, the full dozen of them, from the vase and walked back out to the balcony.

Standing in the dim moonlight, she shredded Whitewater's message into several pieces and let the breeze carry them, dancing, toward the dark sea.

Then, one by one, she tore the petals from the flowers and gave them, too, to the sighing wind. Petal by petal she fed them to the night. When they were all gone, she wished them farewell, knowing she was saying goodbye to her innocence as well. She would never trust anyone again. Not anyone. Not ever.

Josie spent the next week in an odd daze. It was as if her body were in paradise and her mind in limbo, some curiously dim and lifeless region.

Bettina would soon be released and sent to stay for an undetermined time with Mr. Suehiro and his wife. Mr. Suehiro, devoting all his time to ensuring Bettina's freedom, turned Josie over to one of his partners, the youthful-looking Mr. Hongo.

Lewis Hongo, who looked more like a surfing champion than a lawyer, smilingly reassured Josie that no charges would be brought against her. He insisted that it was likley, since Bettina was cooperating so fully with authorities, that she, too, would be spared. The authorities preferred that the two sisters did not meet or talk, however; they didn't want them collaborating on their stories.

Grudgingly Josie agreed, but only because she had no choice. She knew the gentlemanly Mr. Suehiro would take good care of Bettina. Lewis Hongo, who was not only a rising star in the Honolulu legal world, but also a young, handsome and single one, offered to take Josie out for drinks and show her the nightlife of Waikiki. She thanked him politely and said no. She still felt too hurt and hollow to want to be among people and pretend to act normally.

Willis, she was glad to learn, was behind bars, as was the large and frightening Ollie, who was no worse for her having tranquilized him. Of Lucas there was no word. He was missing on Kali Chenshan. Lewis Hongo told Josie that he himself presumed Lucas was dead, but they might never know.

Kana-Puma was still erupting, although its main damage seemed confined to the east side of the island. The volcano's first outburst had been its most violent so far, but no one was sure how long it would continue to display its fireworks: weeks or years. The prevailing winds kept the Mount of Cloudy Gods in a rain of dust and ash much of the time, and kept most planes from landing at the village airstrip. Most of the island's small population was being evacuated.

Josie's one joy was that every morning she went to a special room at the zoo at Kapiolani Park. The room had security guards, and Josie had to have clearance to enter. In the room was the best-kept secret in Hawaii: Moon Flower and Billabong. Both were doing splendidly. Moon Flower had not seemed surprised to awaken and find herself a mother. She took it all in her waddling panda stride. Billabong remained pink, blind—and astonishingly healthy.

Josie was allowed two hours each day with the pandas, but Dr. Hazard would be flying in from Chicago at the end of the week. Then he would take over supervision of the pandas, and Josie was unsure how he would feel about her presence. He had sent her a brief telegram:

Thank you. Cannot tell you extent of my gratitude. Wish I could ask you to return, but as you know, not possible. With combined appreciation and regret,

T. Wallace Hazard

With combined appreciation and regret, she thought sadly. That was how he would always think of her. Her every moment with the pandas became more precious.

She did not know how long she would be allowed to be near them.

The rest of the time Josie kept to herself. She rented a car and toured the island of Oahu one day, but the beautiful scenery seemed like images on a screen, a lovely illusion.

She felt most comfortable at the beach. She swam alone in the blue water; she spread out a towel and sunned for hours on the white sands. Her pallor turned to a honeyed tan, sprinkled with freckles. The sun teased the gold highlights in her auburn hair out of hiding and made them shine.

Men approached her frequently. Coolly she turned them away. Five days passed. When she was not with Lewis Hongo or the pandas, she was in her bikini, alone on the beach, or sitting alone on the terrace of the hotel, sipping pineapple juice and staring out to sea, trying to forget Aaron Whitewater.

He made no move to get in touch with her. He made no attempt to offer an apology or even an explanation. She assumed the vase of white flowers had been supposed to make up for everything. As each day passed, she hated him more and was more bitterly glad she had destroyed the blooms.

On Tuesday, she spent the morning with the pandas. She thought that Billabong was beginning to get his distinctive panda markings: a haze of dark fuzz shadowed his ears and legs, and seemed to give his closed eyes spectacles. She went back to the hotel and changed into her blue-green bikini. She took the heavy terry robe the hotel provided and went to her lonely vigil of sun worship on the beach.

She had no idea who was paying for her stay at the hotel. She supposed it was the FBI's idea of providing a cover story for her being in Hawaii. Lewis Hongo told her that, if anyone asked, she was to say she was on vacation. Well, she thought ironically, strolling down the white sands and listening to the surf, if the FBI wanted to keep her at a luxury hotel, fine. It was her tax money they were spending. She supposed they were paying the attorneys, too. If she was going to be billed for all this in the end, she would simply have to declare bankruptcy. The authorities surely knew she was out of a job. They probably knew what she had in her bank account to the last penny.

She swam only briefly, for the surf was strong. She lay in the sun, trying to let it bake all thought from her head. She spent too much of her time remembering Whitewater and resenting him. At the same time, she remembered, with a curiously deep longing, the days and nights they had been together. Yes, she thought morosely, she had loved him. Why else should she now hate him so thoroughly?

A shadow fell across her body, cutting off her sunlight and her train of thought. She rose on her elbow, putting on her sunglasses so she could stare up at the figure looming over her.

He was tall, broad of shoulder, and his dark hair tossed slightly in the warm breeze. He wore gray slacks, a blazing white shirt and a blue tie.

Whitewater. For the past five days she had rehearsed all the scathing things she would say to him if he dared to show his face. But they all flew from her mind. She stared up at him, her heart pounding madly.

"Miss Talbott?" he asked. He had a suit coat thrown over his shoulder. "My name is Whitewater."

Josie blinked at him. Her racing pulses slowed in disappointment. The man might be Whitewater, but he was not *her* Whitewater. He was tall, but not as intimidatingly tall as Aaron. He was not as heavily muscled, either; his body was well shaped but tended toward leanness. And although he was handsome, he was handsome in a different way.

"David Whitewater," he said, noting her surprise. "My brother wanted me to ask after you. I couldn't get here any sooner. I was in the middle of a trial in Nebraska. Would you care for a drink on the terrace? I'm afraid I'm not exactly dressed for the beach."

He didn't smile. He looked more solemn than his brother, more serious. Josie nodded numbly. Just because Aaron Whitewater was one of the lower life-forms on earth, she had no cause to be rude to his brother. On the other hand, she had no cause to be overjoyed to meet him, either.

She ignored his proffered hand and rose coolly, slipping into her white robe. She gathered up her towel and beach bag and led the way to the terrace.

"How did you find me?" she asked, not bothering to look back at the tall man behind her.

"You weren't in your room. I decided to check the beach. My brother said you were a redhead, and freckles looked great on you. I looked for a redhead with fetching freckles. Yours were the most fetching on the beach. Is this table all right?"

Josie straightened primly, pulling her robe more tightly closed. She let David Whitewater draw out a chair for her. He sat down across from her, loosening his tie. She tossed him a glance that she meant to be cool and appraising. She failed. He was too much like his brother. The memories came tumbling back.

"I've met Mr. Suehiro," David Whitewater said, watching Josie closely. "He seems almost frighteningly competent. He says his partner has handled your . . . problems, shall we call them. Mr. Hongo. I've also met him. He assures me that the authorities want nothing more from you."

"I should hope not," Josie replied, trying to keep the resentment out of her voice. "I just want to know when I can go back to Chicago." Not, she thought, that she had anything to go back to.

"In a few days," David said vaguely. "I've talked to the authorities, too." He signaled the waiter.

"Sounds as if you've had a busy morning," Josie said tightly. His eyes, she noted, were unlike his brother's. They were a startling sky blue in his bronzed face. They held hers without flinching.

"I have," he answered. The waiter appeared and David ordered wine for Josie, coffee for himself. A dove landed boldly on their table and Josie shooed it away.

"My brother—" began David.

"I do not care," Josie interjected acidly, "to discuss your brother. Now or ever. Your brother may sizzle in Hades from now until Judgment Day. And may the devils baste him in boiling oil."

"My brother," he resumed, ignoring her outburst, "was concerned that you and your sister had adequate representation. He insisted on my coming here. He's concerned about you."

"His method of showing his concern was to arrest me," Josie retorted, "and my sister. I'm glad he was concerned. Heaven knows what he would have done to us if he'd felt unfriendly."

David Whitewater set his jaw. He seemed to search inwardly for patience and, at last, to find it. "I can understand your being upset with my brother—"

"Very good. You must be the bright one in the family. Go to the head of the class."

"I understand your attitude," he repeated unflinchingly. "I myself have always looked on Aaron's James Bond streak with distrust. I've always been afraid one of these days he was going to get himself in trouble. I didn't, however, think it would be woman trouble."

"He doesn't have woman trouble," Josie snapped, not glancing at the waiter when he set down their drinks. "He has ethics trouble. Namely, he lacks them."

"His only problem in that department is that he has too many ethics," David snapped back at her. "He's never been afraid to put his life on the line for a principle. Certain property was stolen. He retrieved it at the request of his government."

"He also lied to me," Josie accused. She took a drink of her wine, wishing it would calm her.

"He had no choice," David returned, his blue eyes like cold fire. "He was under orders. You're supposed to be bright. Didn't it ever occur to you that your phone was tapped? Didn't you wonder why nobody beat you up to the top of that mountain?"

"Of course it occurred to me," she admitted unhappily. "I just didn't think anybody knew. And things were happening so fast, I didn't have time to think about it."

"Maybe you didn't want to think about it," he suggested ironically. "Maybe you hoped somebody was listening in, that somebody would take the responsibility out of your hands. Perhaps unconsciously you hoped the authorities would know—and do something."

"Save your psychology for the courtroom," Josie answered with displeasure. But David's words disturbed her. She had secretly wondered the same thing herself in her darkest moments.

"He had to lie to you," David pursued, his expression grim. "Would you have gone with him if you had known the truth?"

"I don't know," she replied truthfully. "I suppose I would have. I wanted...wanted Bettina and Moon Flower."

"He had orders to arrest you, you know. He could hardly tell you that."

She turned her face away. The way the breeze toyed with his dark hair reminded her too much, too achingly of his brother. "Orders," she said bitterly.

"I don't think you understand what kind of man my brother is," he said, an almost deadly quiet in his voice.

"Don't I?"

"Our growing up wasn't exactly easy," David said. "First our mother left. Our father was in the Navy. He traveled a lot. She met someone else. Her new love didn't want a couple of half-breed brats."

She turned back to him. She had never thought of Aaron as a half-breed. He was simply Aaron.

"Our father didn't take it well," David continued. "He dumped us with our grandfather and just disappeared from our lives. He died in Japan. The circumstances were kind of mysterious. I think he was killed in a fight. Aaron was twelve then. I was nine. Six years later our grandfather died, and all I had in the world was an aunt who sent us the little money she could—and a big brother who'd stand up to the devil himself."

Josie stared at the tabletop. The passionate admiration in David's voice hurt. She didn't want to respect Aaron Whitewater. She didn't dare.

"And my brother made something of himself," David continued relentlessly. "He started as a guide, became partner to a hunting outfitter, and in three years, he owned the whole business. In six, he owned two more—and the biggest consulting agency for hunters in the Midwest. He could have rested on his laurels, but he used his time and money to become the best damn hunter in this country. My Aunt Cora saved money for me to go to college, and Aaron paid her back every dime, with interest. And put me through law school. Every year he sends enough money back to Rosebud to make sure other kids get to go to college. And in his spare time, he sticks his neck out for his country. Don't tell me he doesn't have any ethics, lady. Do me a favor and just don't."

Josie glanced up at him. His face was taut and his blue eyes flashed with emotion. The set of his mouth was exactly the same as Aaron's when he was being stubborn. "You must be dynamite in the courtroom," she said softly. She fingered the stem of her wineglass. "But your brother didn't just lie to me. He lied *about* me. I wouldn't call that moral."

He gave a bitter little laugh. "I don't know what happened between the two of you on that island," he said, lowering his dark brows. "I don't care."

"Nothing happened between us," Josie insisted. But had they been there any longer, things would have happened, and she knew it.

David shrugged, his face impassive. "He told the authorities he slept with you. Is that true?"

"Yes," she answered in confusion, "but—"

"Whether he made love to you is beside the point," David uttered between his teeth. "The point is that he said he did. That got him into some heavy trouble with the Bureau. It also assured they'll never try to bring any pressure to bear on you. You could turn around and scream entrapment and abuse, and any number of other unpleasant things. He got you off the hook. Or hoped he did. He sent me to make sure.''

Josie looked at him without comprehension. A muscle played in his lean jaw. His eyes met hers in challenge.

"You mean," she asked softly, "that he did it to protect me? To make sure that they wouldn't hold me?"

"No jury in America would convict you after what you've done," David said, his voice heavy with irony. "And no lawyer would even try to prosecute you if he believed on top of everything else that one of the government's agents had seduced you. Aaron was supposed to get you to the top of Ra-Koma, not get into your lingerie, excuse my frankness."

Josie stared for a long moment at the intense man across from her. She gave a disbelieving little laugh. "You really are quite a lawyer," she scoffed. "You almost had me believing you. What a line! He tells lies about your virtue, madame, but only to protect you from greater harm. Clever. Not credible, but clever."

"Believe what you want," David Whitewater answered, flashing her an eloquent glance. "He's put his standing with the Bureau in jeopardy for your sake. Accept it or don't."

"If he's so terribly concerned, where's he been?" challenged Josie. "Why isn't he trying out this impossible explanation himself? Where's he been since he...since he arrested us?"

"If you don't know, I can't tell you," he replied curtly.

"What do you mean, you can't tell me?" she demanded.

"I can't tell you because he wouldn't tell me," he answered. "He said you were the only person who'd know. Are you saying he didn't inform you, either?"

The envelope, Josie thought, a sinking void within her. She remembered the pieces of the envelope flying out toward the sea on the night wind. "He...he left me a message. I destroyed it. I never read it."

David Whitewater looked at her in accusing silence. "I haven't heard from him since that night, Miss Talbott," he said at last. "I'm worried about him. Now you tell me you've destroyed my only hope of locating him. Thank you. Thank you very much."

Sorrow and confusion warred in Josie's mind. "You mean... But he couldn't just disappear. He had to work with the authorities. He—"

"He's not on these islands, Miss Talbot," David stated flatly. "And the authorities aren't sure where he is—exactly."

Josie stared at him expectantly, watching the sunlight glance off his dark hair. "What do you mean—exactly?" she questioned, fear starting to ice her heart.

"We think he's gone back to Kali Chenshan," David answered, his expression solemn. "Back to the island."

"But he couldn't!" Josie objected. "It's too dangerous there. Almost everyone's evacuated. Planes can hardly land. Nobody knows what that volcano's going to do next. It's hellish there."

"I'm aware of that," David answered. "But you wished my brother in hell, didn't you? Perhaps you've got your wish."

"But why?" Josie begged, not understanding. "Why would he do such a dangerous thing?"

"Your sister's little friend," David replied with distaste. "Lucas Panpaxis. We think Aaron went back to see if he could find him. If he's alive. Not that he's worth saving."

"But . . ." Josie protested, clutching her robe around her more tightly. In spite of the sunshine she was suddenly cold. "But why? Did the Bureau send him? How could they?"

"Nobody sent him. He went on his own," David replied stonily.

"Why?" Josie asked, as chilled as if the sun had disappeared forever. "Why would he do such a thing?"

David Whitewater's dark brows drew together. He gave Josie a long measuring look. "Maybe," he declared sarcastically, "he did it out of a sense of ethics. But I forget. He has no ethics, has he?"

He stood up, taking the check and tossing a tip beside his untouched coffee cup. "Have you been reading any papers, Miss Talbott? Listening to the news today, or watching it on television?"

She shook her head, staring up at him, watching the way the wind stirred his hair. At that moment, his resemblance to Aaron was almost too strong for her to bear.

"About the time I was interviewing your lawyer," David said, his face obdurate, "the handsome and charming Mr. Hongo—and you were sunning so prettily on this beach—Kana-Puma erupted so violently they think the entire mountain range may rupture. The whole island may be torn in half. And if it is, nobody there is going to live through it."

She stood so swiftly that she knocked her wineglass over. It rolled off the table and shattered on the tiles of the terrace. She hardly noticed. She gripped the collar of her robe until her knuckles whitened. She was pale beneath her tan.

"You mean," she whispered hoarsely, "he could die?"

He regarded her coldly. "That's precisely what I mean. And you know, somehow I have the feeling that, if he did go back to that damned island, he went for you—maybe to prove to you he's not the bastard you think. But don't worry. You're taken care of. He made me promise to see to that. That you'd be all right. He's got you the best lodgings money could buy—and the best lawyers. And I'm here to ensure everything goes swimmingly for you. Good day, Miss Talbott."

He left her standing there. She turned to watch him stride toward the entrance of the hotel. Behind the building, rising in the eastern sky, was a faint smoky-looking mist.

Volcanic dust from Kana-Puma, she thought hopelessly, coloring the sky so that it could be seen even from here. Was David right? Had Whitewater gone back because of her? Had he written that to her the night he sent the flowers? What had he wanted to tell her?

She had torn up the flowers and sent them flying away on the night winds. And she had torn up his words, as well. His precious words. She would never know what he had said.

She stood, cold as ice in the brilliant afternoon sunlight. "Whitewater," she said softly, as if his name were a prayer that could protect him.

A waiter, drawn by the glass she had broken, was at her side. He touched her elbow hesitantly. "Are you all right, miss?" he asked.

She did not even know he was there. She stared at the rising cloud in the distance. "Whitewater," she whispered again.

CHAPTER TEN

BACK IN HER ROOM, Josie moved about blindly, automatically. She called Lewis Hongo, who grudgingly admitted he did not know where Aaron Whitewater was. Probed further, he finally acknowledged that the Bureau, believing Mr. Whitewater had taken certain matters into his own hands, was most unhappy with him.

"Yes, yes, all right," Lewis Hongo at last confessed under the merciless barrage of Josie's questioning. Aaron Whitewater was paying her hotel bills and her attorney's fees as well as Bettina's—the firm was pledged to secrecy on this point, but she obviously knew the truth. Now would she let him alone? Please? He had to be in court.

She hung up the phone feeling helpless and exhausted. She turned on the large color television and watched for news of the latest eruption of Kana-Puma. It came as a special report in the early afternoon.

Josie, still in her robe and feeling cold to the marrow of her bones, sat on the huge bed and watched. Footage shot from a news helicopter showed flames spewing from the island into the sky. A pillar of dark smoke and dust billowed straight up into the air like an accusing finger.

A rain of cinders drove the news helicopter back, dipping and weaving. The island grew smaller in the distance, sparks and flares of fire dancing from it.

Refugees from the threatened Kali Chenshan were interviewed. Some spoke of chunks of flame falling from the sky, of blasts like cannon fire rending the air. A creeping wall of lava was moving eastward on the island, and if it reached far enough, it would change the island's shoreline. Parts of the island were being buried in ash.

Hunched on the bed, Josie felt hope dying within her. She was briefly uplifted when the reporter interviewed both Horace and Berke Coelho.

Horace said stoically that he intended to go back to his ranch when this was over. "I happen to live in a place that explodes a bit from time to time," he explained with perfect dignity. "It is, nevertheless, my home. I will rebuild whatever needs rebuilding."

Berke Coelho was not so sanguine. "I don't know," he said, shaking his dark head when the reporter questioned him. "It may be time for me to move on. A man can't fight the volcano forever. Who knows how long this could last? Years, maybe."

"You were among the last people known to have left Kali Chenshan," the reporter said to Berke Coelho.

"We were the last to leave by air," Berke stated. "We had to hose the ash off the wings before we could take off. It's so bad now, I don't know if it's possible for anybody to take off."

"Are there other people still on the island?" the reporter persisted.

Berke Coelho swallowed and looked into the camera. He nodded. "Yes." He nodded again, as if words failed him. He seemed to gather his self-control with difficulty. "I know of one for sure. A hunter who went into the interior five days ago. His plane was still at the airstrip when we left. It was disappearing under the ash. It was being buried."

Buried, Josie thought with a sickening sense of finality. A hunter. Five days ago. Whitewater. Somewhere on that ash-swept, fire-spouting hell. Trapped. And for what? For Lucas Panpaxis, who had started this whole nightmare in the first place.

She used the remote-control switch to turn off the television. She sat on the bed. She remembered lying in Whitewater's naked arms in the paradise of Kali Chenshan. She remembered his hands on her body, making it sing with life, when he kissed her in the pool on the side of the Mount of Cloudy Gods.

Now paradise was in flames and Whitewater was gone. He might be gone forever. She buried her face in her hands. She sobbed. She had not cried so since she was a child.

She was so drowned in grief that at first she didn't hear the pounding on her door. She rose, not caring that she couldn't control her tears. She flung open the door. "What is it?" she demanded, and was about to tell the intruder to go away.

Then she looked up into the intent and somber blue eyes of David Whitewater. "I just saw the television report," he said grimly. "I thought you should know. It sounds like—"

"I know what it sounds like," Josie cried, bursting into fresh tears. "It sounds like he's dead. He can't be dead! He can't be. He just...can't..."

David stared down at her for a moment in consternation. "You...you really do care for him?" he asked doubtfully.

"I love him!" Josie flung back, wiping her eyes. "How could I have been so angry with him if I didn't love him? He lied to me, he deceived me, he even arrested me, but yes, heaven help me, I love him."

David looked sad and uncomfortable. His sky-blue eyes radiated reluctant sympathy. He stepped into her room and closed the door behind him. He put his arm around her shoulder to soothe the uncontrollable shudders that were beginning to shake her.

"Maybe we should wait together," he said in a tight voice. "I don't think Aaron would want me to leave you alone. I'll stay if you want."

"Yes," Josie gasped, burying her face in her hands again. "Please stay."

THEY KEPT A TENSE VIGIL together. David left word for his calls to be transferred to her room. He made Josie get out of her wet bathing suit and damp robe, shower and put on fresh clothes. He called room service and had a meal delivered, which he made her eat.

He himself seemed to exist only on black coffee and an occasional cigarette. "I gave these up years ago," he mused quietly, examining a cigarette before he lit it. "But tobacco used to be sacred to the Indians—used as kind of an offering. I don't know. Maybe part of me believes in magic. If I breathe fire, Aaron won't have to." He inhaled deeply.

Josie, dressed in her turquoise-colored shirtwaist, sat on the bed, plucking nervously at the bedspread. "I tore up his flowers," she said unhappily. "It was stupid of me. I was just so full of anger. And hurt. But I shouldn't have ruined the flowers. They were the most beautiful flowers I've ever seen."

David ground out his cigarette as if its taste offended him or he no longer believed in its magic. "You'd been through a lot, Josie," he offered. "Don't blame yourself. I was too quick to lash out. We both acted as we did because we care for Aaron. And since we both care about him, we might as well be friends."

"Yes," murmured Josie. "I could use a friend."

But what she really wanted was Whitewater back.

They watched the evening news and the late-night news. They stayed up together until midnight, when a sudden rainstorm came up and began to pound at the glass of the sliding doors.

"I'm going back to my room," David informed her at last. "I'll see you in the morning. If nobody's heard anything from Aaron by then, I'm going to hire a helicopter and try to scout Kali Chenshan myself."

He stood, and Josie stood, as well. "He wouldn't want you to do that," she stated, because she knew it was the truth.

"Josie," he said gently, "somebody has to do it."

"Then I'm going with you," she said stubbornly. "At least I know part of the island. That's more than you do."

"No," he answered firmly, and once again his implacability reminded her of Aaron. "You can't leave Hawaii. And if Aaron wouldn't want me going to Chenshan, I know he wouldn't want you there."

"We'll argue about it tomorrow," she said tiredly.

He gave her a tight little smile, chucked her under the chin in a slightly awkward brotherly gesture. "An old poet used to come visit my grandfather at the reservation. Once my Aunt Cora was there. She was going through some kind of trouble. She didn't like the people she worked for, but she thought she owed it to their children—or maybe it was their grandchildren—to stay. She didn't know what to do. So the old poet said to her, 'You've got to have trust in two things: courage and love, lady. Courage and love.' You, too, Josie, must trust in them."

"I'll try," she answered, her voice strained.

"Good night," he said.

"Good night," she answered. He left her alone.

She went to the sliding doors and opened them. She stared out at the darkness and pouring rain. Was it raining, she wondered, on Kali Chenshan, in the Mala Lui Valley, on the Mount of Cloudy Gods? Were the fires of Kana-Puma still burning in the rain? And was Whitewater still alive out there somewhere in the darkness and the storm?

Not so much as a star shone in answer. Only the rain hissed, speaking a message she could not translate.

She crossed her arms and looked up at the black sky. "Courage and love, lady," she thought, closing her eyes. A hot tear slid down her cheek. "Courage and love."

JOSIE SPENT THE MORNING with her attorney, Lewis Hongo, who was, for a change, frowning and sullen. Mr. Suehiro had learned that Lewis had revealed that Whitewater was paying the bills. At this very moment Mr. Suehiro was devising an appropriate punishment, probably consisting of presenting Lewis with the worst, dullest and most impossible cases coming through the firm's doors for the next six months.

"Now," Lewis told Josie, his darkly handsome face glum. "The official story is going to be this: the Chicago Zoo expected trouble with Moon Flower's pregnancy. They were flying her to Hawaii, where your people would meet with Dr. Mitsui, a zoologist from Tokyo and a scholar on the birth problems of the panda. There was an attempted hijacking of the plane carrying Moon Flower. It was foiled by federal agents. During the attempt, however, the plane was forced somewhat off course, and the cub was born, unexpectedly, over international waters."

"Why such an elaborate lie?" Josie asked rebelliously. "The truth has to come out eventually when Willis and Ollie go to trial."

"We all know that," Lewis Hongo growled. "We want to minimize the danger the animal was in for as long as possible. As we've told you, we want no copycat crimes. By delaying the truth, we give zoos a chance to beef up their security systems. And for as long as possible, we save face. We can see that the news is broken diplomatically. This could have been an international incident."

Josie turned from the handsome, sulky young man in distaste. "There have been too many lies already," she said, staring out his office window. It was a gray day. Outside the palm trees bobbed their fronds in the misty wind.

"It's a matter of security," Lewis replied testily. "And if the Bureau can, it will keep your name and Whitewater's out of it completely. You are under government orders to keep quiet—unless otherwise instructed. It's the least you can do. You're getting off very lightly, you know."

Josie gave him a bitter little smile. She didn't feel she had gotten off lightly. She picked up her clutch purse from Lewis's desk. She rose. "Goodbye, Mr. Hongo," she said with a sigh, her patience gone.

He glared up at her. "Do you understand what I've just told you, Josie?" he demanded. His boyishly attractive face was petulant.

"Perfectly," she snapped back. "I just don't much care any longer." She turned on her heel and started toward the office door.

"You'd better care," he warned. "This firm has gone to a lot of trouble and expense to see that you're protected. To say nothing of your sister..."

Josie opened the door and left, shutting it behind her with more force than necessary. All she cared about was Whitewater. "Official" and "authorized" versions of the truth didn't matter. She was sick unto death of lies, no matter how fine a purpose they served.

She went into the drizzly street and hailed a cab to take her to the zoo. She settled into the back seat and put her fingertips to her throbbing forehead. The truth, she thought unhappily. Perhaps she would never know the truth.

She had no idea what Whitewater's note had said that night she destroyed the orchids. Perhaps it was a simple apology, that was all. Perhaps he had seen to her welfare, not because he loved her, but simply because, as David said, Aaron Whitewater was a moral man. He had been forced to lie to her, seemingly to betray her, and he had been trying to make up for it. She might never know.

And why had he gone after Lucas? she fretted helplessly. Surely David was wrong; there was no reason Whitewater would return to the island for Josie's sake. He must have simply disliked leaving Lucas behind. It had been his responsibility to take him into custody, and he had failed. He had returned to do the job correctly. He always tried to do the right thing.

She had spent the past few days looking into her heart about Whitewater's hunting, as well. She recognized her feelings for what they were: prejudice, not conviction. It was not the sportsmen who threatened wildlife, not men like Whitewater. Most sportsmen treated animals as a resource, one they were dedicated to keeping renewed. Commercial hunters, those who slew seals and whales, were the problem, as well as those who trapped thousands of wild animals each year for the exotic pet trade or research.

The great growth of human civilization was in itself responsible. The panda had not been hunted nearly to extinction; rather, their feeding grounds had been taken over by humans, nearly destroyed, and that was what most seriously endangered them. But she might never have the chance to tell Whitewater that she understood now. Tears blurred her vision.

The zoo and the park were located beside Diamond Head. Josie hurried to the room where the pandas were being kept. Moon Flower and Billy seemed the only stable, dependable things in a world where truth and falsehood shifted daily. Soon they would be taken from her. She smiled sadly through the bars at her beautiful ebony-and-white Moon Flower.

The big panda lay on her side and cocked her head slightly at Josie, as if to say, "Why so unhappy? Look at our beautiful baby." She had Billy cradled in the crook of her elbow. Today his little mask seemed darker. He was turning into a miniature replica of his exotic mother.

Josie's reverie was interrupted when someone tapped her shoulder. "Miss? Miss?" said a young woman in a white smock. "There is a gentleman here to see you. A Mr. Whitewater."

Josie spun around to face the woman, her heart leaping happily. The surge of hope coursing through her made her temporarily giddy.

"A Mr. David Whitewater," the woman continued. "He says it's urgent."

Josie's heart dropped back to normal speed, then seemed to slow to a mournful half cadence. David, she realized, her thoughts deadening. They had breakfasted together in grim silence. He had insisted on flying to Kali Chenshan himself, and had flatly refused to let Josie go with him. She glanced at her watch. It was almost noon—he should have left by now. Unless he had heard something.

Something's happened, she thought, and moved quickly out of the guarded panda room, mechanically removing her clearance badge and thrusting it into her purse. She was nearly running as she left the building. Half-insensible with fear, yet tortured by impossible hopes, she literally ran into David when he stepped out of the shadow of a palm tree.

The gray wind gusted slightly about them. His ice-blue eyes stared down into her frightened ones. He said nothing. But she knew. The expression on his face told her everything. Something had happened to Whitewater.

She was silenced by horror for a long moment. She shook her head vigorously, denying the ultimate dread. "He's not..." she began, looking up defiantly at David. "He's not..."

"He's very badly off, Josie," David said, his face taut. "He got Lucas. And somehow the two of them made it off the island just before the big blow yesterday. By canoe. They got to one of the smaller islands. Lucas was knocked around in the surf, but he's otherwise nearly unscathed. They've got him in the hospital. But Aaron...Aaron's hurt badly, Josie. They're bringing them both to the hospital in Honolulu. I've come to take you there.''

He ushered her toward the parking lot and his rented car. She gnawed worriedly at the inside of her cheek. "How bad is he, David?" she finally managed to ask, her voice choked.

He opened the door for her and paused, looking down at her. "He's got a fifty-fifty chance," he stated, his gaze not wavering. "But he got badly scorched by the ash. Even if he makes it, they're worried about his eyes. He might be blinded.

"No," Josie breathed. She sank into the car seat numbly. Not his eyes. Not that, she thought. Not his hawklike hunter's eyes. He'd rather be dead than lose his sight. Not that. Not that.

"No," SAID the wiry little gray-haired nurse firmly. Josie and David most certainly could not see Mr. Whitewater. Guards were posted outside his door and the orders were clear: no one, except hospital personnel and investigators, were to be allowed inside. Mr. Whitewater was wavering back and forth between consciousness and unconsciousness, anyway. He should not be disturbed.

"Lady, we're family," snarled David, and for the first time Josie realized he might be every bit as formidable as his brother. "You let us in that room or I start making new doors in these walls."

Josie recognized the two men walking toward them. They were the agents who had taken her and Bettina into custody. The taller of the two flipped open his wallet and showed his identification to David. "We'll arrange for you to see your brother," he said. "I have some information for you. Would you step aside with me a moment, please?"

"And I want you to come with me," said the shorter man to Josie. He was the one to whom she had been handcuffed. His little gray eyes glittered, and for some reason a smug smile played around his lips. He took her by the arm.

"What . . . ?" Josie asked in confusion. The hard-faced little agent was leading her away, down the hall. She turned, looking to David for assistance, but he was deep in conversation with the other man, frowning hard.

"Just come with me, Miss Talbott," ordered the agent, leading her down a hallway. "We have someone who wants to talk to you."

I don't believe this, Josie thought in terrified bafflement. Whitewater was hurt, maybe blinded, maybe dying, and she was being arrested again. The world had turned to nightmare.

"In here, please," he said, opening a door that looked like any other door. Except when he opened it, Aaron Whitewater was standing there, buttoning up a brick-red shirt that was too small for him.

She looked at him. He had a bruise on one high cheekbone and a slight cut slashing through one dark eyebrow. There was a bandage around his left wrist, and a thick one around his left ankle. But he was alive. He was standing. He was fine.

She felt her knees buckle. He stepped forward quickly and caught her in his arms. "Hello," he said, his brown-black eyes scanning her face hungrily. "How are things?"

The arms around her were strong and real. They held her up and she realized being in their safety again. He smelled of soap and shaving cream. She looked up at him in dazed disbelief. "I thought you were dying...they said...David's here...they told David you might be blinded...you had only a fifty-fifty chance of pulling through."

"I'm sure the two of you will excuse me," the short agent said dryly and shut the door.

"As Mark Twain said, the reports of my death are greatly exaggerated," he said softly. "I'm back, Josie. I got Lucas out for you, and I'm back."

The strength was returning into her body now, and joy was flooding her veins. She could stand again, but she didn't move away from his arms. She could only gaze raptly up at him. He didn't seem able to take his eyes from her, either. His dark gaze devoured her.

"Oh, Whitewater," she whispered, "why did you go back? Why on earth?"

"I told you why," he said huskily. "I left you a letter. The night before I went back."

"I didn't read it," she replied, tears rising in her eyes. "I was so angry, I felt so betrayed...."

He drew back slightly. "You never read it?"

She shook her head, ashamed. "I tore it up," she whispered, turning her face from him.

"Thank God," he stated. "Then tell me that's why you didn't call me that night."

"Call you?" she asked in confusion, turning her face up to him again. He put lean fingers under her chin, traced the outline of her lower lip with his thumb. The gesture was both tender and sensual. Josie felt herself dissolving like dew at his touch.

"Josie," he murmured, taking her face between his hands. "I had orders to arrest you when we got Moon Flower back. It was the hardest thing I've ever done. The look on your face is burned into my heart, I swear. I never want to see that look again. I asked you to forgive me. I told you I was going back for Lucas because I knew how sickened you'd been that I left him there. I thought, just maybe, if I could find him, you'd understand how I'd felt. That I'd do anything for your forgiveness."

"Oh, Whitewater," she said, biting her lower lip, "I didn't want you to do that—take your life in your hands."

"I told you more than that, Josie," he muttered, his thumbs tracing the delicate curve of her jawline. "I said more in that letter than I've ever said to any woman. Including all the reasons I knew it could never work between us, all the reasons I thought you'd use—that I'd deceived you, that I was an arrogant bastard, that we came from two different worlds and believed in altogether different things. But that if you thought there was a chance—so much as a ghost of a chance—to call me. And then I knew I could walk through all the fires of Kana-Puma for you. But you didn't call. And I couldn't blame you."

"I never knew," she said, smiling up at him in spite of her tears.

"And if you had known?" he asked solemnly, staring deep into her eyes. "If you had known, what would you have done?"

She shook her head in perplexity. She bit her lip again. "I don't know, Whitewater," she answered truthfully. "Nobody ever hurt me the way you did. At that point I don't know what I would have said."

His fingers were twined in the tendrils of her darkly fiery hair. "Do I even have the right to ask you for an answer now? I've tried to prove to you, Josie, that I do care about you. Maybe more than anything."

"I knew you'd lied to me, even lied about me," she offered, trying to explain the tumult of her feelings during the past days.

"I hated lying to you," he said passionately, bringing his face closer to hers. "As for lying about you, I wanted to protect you. The Bureau thinks I seduced you. I also took matters into my own hands and went after Lucas when they wouldn't try. They'll never want me to work for them again. Fine. I don't want to. It's cost me too much. I'm through. And if I didn't make love to you, it wasn't because I didn't want to. I never wanted anything so badly in my life."

She wasn't sure she'd heard him correctly. She was afraid to ask him to say it again for fear she'd misunderstood. "When...when David said he thought you'd gone back to the island," she murmured unhappily, "and when they told him you were hurt so badly, that you might even be blinded—" Her pent-up emotions overcame her. "Oh, Whitewater," she said, tears streaming down her face, "how could you do such a thing?"

"Josie, Josie," he comforted, wiping the tears away with his hand. "It had to be done. I rented a plane and flew back to the island. I couldn't land on the Mount of Cloudy Gods because of the fallout from Kana-Puma, so I had to use the airstrip and take the way in we took again, then try to track him. It was a devil of a job. But I found him—not in the best of shape, but alive. Then it was a question of getting him out. We made it to the west shore and found a canoe. Things felt like they were going to break loose, so I tried to make it to one of the smaller islands."

"How...why..." Josie asked, her voice choked, "did they say you were hurt?"

"Lucas was in bad shape," he repeated, still holding her face as if to assure her he was really there. "I mostly carried him down the mountain over my shoulder. In the canoe he started having the shakes. I put my shirt and bush vest on him. I never thought about my identification being in the vest. We made it within half a mile of another island when Lucas came back to consciousness. He thrashed around and pitched us both out of the canoe. By the time I got hold of him, the boat was swept away. I had to swim half a mile towing the little weasel. I got banged up in the surf. I made it and I got him ashore, and I guess I passed out. A farmer found us. At any rate, by that time Lucas had accidentally been identified as me, and the news had been radioed here. It isn't quite straightened out yet. But the doctors tell me he's going to make it. And he'll see. Maybe not as well as he used to, but he'll see."

"Oh, Whitewater," she said helplessly, "are you really all right? I'm not just dreaming this?"

"I'm all right," he insisted, his eyes intent on her. "I'm back. I'm here. Josie, can you ever forgive me for what I did to you?"

"Forgive you?" she echoed weakly. She had forgiven him, it seemed, an eternity ago.

"Josie," he said with an earnestness that was almost frightening, "I'll do anything for you. I'll even give up hunting. I...I talked to Berke Coelho once about starting a chain of charter fishing boats here in Honolulu. Could you live here, do you think, in Hawaii? With me?"

"With you?" she asked, her breathing shallow. Her heart gave a surge of joyous disbelief.

"With me," he repeated, gazing down at her with barely restrained desire. "Marry me, Josie. I thought I was a lone wolf. I was wrong. I'm like all the other creatures of nature. I need a mate. I need you. I love you. And I want you with every atom of my being."

"Yes," she breathed, and closed her eyes happily as he bent to kiss her. Their mouths met with both gentleness and hunger, and desire flared through Josie with the life-giving brightness of the sun.

She wrapped her arms around his neck, and he swept her against him so tightly that her body seemed to merge with his. He kissed her until once more she felt faint. She gasped, amazed and delighted by the intensity of her feelings.

"I think," he muttered, nuzzling her ear warmly, "that under the circumstances you should call me Aaron."

"Aaron," she said happily. He kissed her ear and then her cheek and then the tip of her nose.

"I know some people at the Honolulu Zoo," he said. "They ought to be delighted to get a new zoologist who's beautiful as well as brainy. That is, if you want to work. Maybe you'd rather stay home and have kids or something. Whatever you want, Josie. I'll build you a house overlooking the sea. I'm going to treat you like a queen, I swear."

She smiled up at him. "You don't have to give up hunting. I'm ready to forfeit the battle. I couldn't take that away from you."

"It doesn't matter, Josie," he insisted, and bent to kiss her again. "You're what matters."

He kissed her, making her soul a part of his own. "Let's get out of here," he said, "and back to the hotel. And I suppose I should ask you how the pandas are."

Josie had completely forgotten about the pandas. "Fine," she said raggedly, coming back to herself slightly. "They're fine. Shouldn't we tell your brother...?"

"One of the agents told him," he assured her. "Besides, I don't need my little brother right now. He'd just be in the way, like little brothers often are. Let's go to the hotel. Now. We have a ceremony to perform."

She looked up at him in puzzlement. "A ceremony?"

One straight dark brow arched wickedly. "That volcano." He smiled. "Kana-Puma. It's still blowing its top. We've got to stop it."

"Stop it? How?" She smoothed back a lock of his dark hair.

He kissed her lips lightly. "Everybody knows there's only one way to stop a volcano. Sacrifice a virgin. Any volunteers?"

She laughed and locked her arms more tightly around his neck. "I volunteer," she said happily.

"Then I," he murmured, nibbling on her ear, "will do everything in my power to help. But I warn you. It's a long ceremony. And a very elaborate one."

"Then we'd better get on with it," she whispered against his throat.

"Right," he said. "And I'll see that you like it. I intend to make you happy. After all, it's my job."

"Your job?" she teased.

"For the rest of my life," he said.

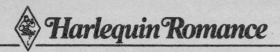 **Harlequin Romance**

Coming Next Month

#3001 UNCONDITIONAL LOVE Claudia Jameson
Coralie's new life in Salisbury is disturbed when Jake Samuels and
his son arrive and Jake offers her a decorating commission. Coralie
knows she can handle the arrogant Jake, but she's convinced
something's wrong in the Samuels household.

#3002 SEND IN THE CLOWN Patricia Knoll
Kathryn, as her alter ego Katydid the Clown, had been adored by
thousands. But as Reid Darwin's temporary personal assistant life is
no circus. What did she have to do to win even a word of praise
from her toughest critic?

#3003 BITTERSWEET PURSUIT Margaret Mayo
Charley isn't looking for romance—she just wants to find
her father. Yet thrown into constant contact with explorer
Braden Quest, who clearly opposes her presence on the jungle
expedition in Peru, Charley is aware of the intense feelings sparking
between them....

#3004 PARADISE FOR TWO Betty Neels
Prudence doesn't regret giving up her own plans to accompany
her godmother to Holland. She finds her surroundings and her
hostess charming. However, she can't understand why the arrogant
Dr. Haso ter Brons Huizinga dislikes her—and tells herself she
doesn't care!

#3005 CROCODILE CREEK Valerie Parv
Keri knows returning to the Champion cattle station can mean
trouble—yet her job as a ranger for Crocodile Task Force requires it.
Meeting Ben Champion again is a risk she must take—but it proves
more than she'd bargained for!

#3006 STILL TEMPTATION Angela Wells
Verona is happy to accompany her young friend Katrina home to
Crete, but her excitement is dampened by Katrina's domineering
brother, Andreas, who expected a middle-aged chaperone, not an
attractive young woman. Suddenly Verona's anticipated holiday
turns into a battle of wills....

Available in September wherever paperback books are sold,
or through Harlequin Reader Service:

In the U.S.
901 Fuhrmann Blvd.
P.O. Box 1397
Buffalo, N.Y. 14240-1397

In Canada
P.O. Box 603
Fort Erie, Ontario
L2A 5X3

SWEEPSTAKES RULES & REGULATIONS

NO PURCHASE NECESSARY TO ENTER OR RECEIVE A PRIZE

1. To enter and join the Reader Service, check off the "YES" box on your Sweepstakes Entry Form and return to Harlequin Reader Service. If you do not wish to join the Reader Service but wish to enter the Sweepstakes only, check off the "NO" box on your Sweepstakes Entry Form. Incomplete and/or inaccurate entries are ineligible for that section or sections(s) of prizes. Not responsible for mutilated or unreadable entries or inadvertent printing errors. Mechanically reproduced entries are null and void. Be sure to also qualify for the Bonus Sweepstakes. See rule #3 on how to enter.

2. Either way, your unique Sweepstakes number will be compared against the list of winning numbers generated at random by the computer. In the event that all prizes are not claimed, random drawings will be held from all entries received from all presentations to award all unclaimed prizes. All cash prizes are payable in U.S. funds. This is in addition to any free, surprise or mystery gifts that might be offered. The following prizes are offered: *Grand Prize (1) $1,000,000 Annuity; First Prize (1) $35,000; Second Prize (1) $10,000; Third Prize (3) $5,000; Fourth Prize (10) $1,000; Fifth Prize (25) $500; Sixth Prize (5,000) $5.
   * This Sweepstakes contains a Grand Prize offering of a $1,000,000 annuity. Winner may elect to receive $25,000 a year for 40 years without interest; totalling $1,000,000 or $350,000 in one cash payment. Entrants may cancel Reader Service at any time without cost or obligation to buy.

3. Extra Bonus Prize: This presentation offers two extra bonus prizes valued at $30,000 each to be awarded in a random drawing from all entries received. To qualify, scratch off the silver on your Lucky Keys. If the registration numbers match, you are eligible for the prize offering.

4. Versions of this Sweepstakes with different graphics will be offered in other mailings or at retail outlets by Torstar Corp. and its affiliates. This promotion is being conducted under the supervision of Marden-Kane, Inc., an independent judging organization. By entering this Sweepstakes, each entrant accepts and agrees to be bound by these rules and the decisions of the judges, which shall be final and binding. Odds of winning in the random drawing are dependent upon the total number of entries received. Taxes, if any, are the sole responsibility of the winners. Prizes are nontransferable. All entries must be received by March 31, 1990. The drawing will take place on or about April 30, 1990 at the offices of Marden-Kane, Inc., Lake Success, N.Y.

5. This offer is open to residents of the U.S., United Kingdom and Canada, 18 years or older, except employees of Torstar Corp., its affiliates, subsidiaries, Marden-Kane and all other agencies and persons connected with conducting this Sweepstakes. All Federal, State and local laws apply. Void wherever prohibited or restricted by law.

6. Winners will be notified by mail and may be required to execute an affidavit of eligibility and release, which must be returned within 14 days after notification. Canadian winners will be required to answer a skill-testing question. Winners consent to the use of their name, photograph and/or likeness for advertising and publicity in conjunction with this or similar promotions, without additional compensation.

7. For a list of our most current major prize winners, send a stamped, self-addressed envelope to: Winners List, c/o Marden-Kane, Inc., P.O. Box 701, Sayreville, N.J. 08871.

If Sweepstakes entry form is missing, please print your name and address on a 3″ × 5″ piece of plain paper and send to:

In the U.S.	In Canada
Sweepstakes Entry	Sweepstakes Entry
901 Fuhrmann Blvd.	P.O. Box 609
P.O. Box 1867	Fort Erie, Ontario
Buffalo, NY 14269-1867	L2A 5X3